'Th... ...ve
the... ...n
use that until...

The generosity ... ...nt
to weep. The last thing she'd been looking
forward to was trudging around the village
with her flowery suitcase.

'That would be fantastic,' she told him
gratefully.

He paused in the kitchen doorway and, as if he
hadn't been dismissive enough, said, 'Let me
know when you want to go across there and
I'll take you on a short guided tour.'

'I'm ready now,' she said meekly, keen to hide
away from his reluctant hospitality.

'OK. So go and sort out what food you want
to take with you and I'll bring your case
down. The sooner you're settled in there the
better you'll feel—even though it will only be
for the one night.'

And the happier you will be on both counts,
she thought. *Count one because it is only for
one night, and count two because you will
have your privacy back. But you will still
have to endure my presence at the surgery,
Dr Lawrence, and you could be in for a
surprise, as my sparkle has only been dimmed,
not extinguished...*

Hello Dear Reader.

Once again we meet the Doctors of Swallowbrook Farm Practice in my second book of the series. In the first we had Libby and Nathan's story, and now we meet Ruby and Hugo who find a very special kind of love amongst the lakes and fells that surround a delightful village.

I do hope that you will enjoy reading about the doctors of this country practice once more, and maybe we will meet again in books three and four.

With very best regards

Abigail Gordon

SPRING PROPOSAL IN SWALLOWBROOK

BY
ABIGAIL GORDON

MILLS & BOON

All the characters in this book have no existence outside the imagination of the author, and have no relation whatsoever to anyone bearing the same name or names. They are not even distantly inspired by any individual known or unknown to the author, and all the incidents are pure invention.

First published in Great Britain 2012
by Mills & Boon, an imprint of Harlequin (UK) Limited.
Harlequin (UK) Limited, Eton House,
18-24 Paradise Road, Richmond, Surrey TW9 1SR

© Abigail Gordon 2012

ISBN: 978 0 263 89148 5

Harlequin (UK) policy is to use papers that are natural, renewable and recyclable products and made from wood grown in sustainable forests. The logging and manufacturing process conform to the legal environmental regulations of the country of origin.

Printed and bound in Spain
by Blackprint CPI, Barcelona

Abigail Gordon loves to write about the fascinating combination of medicine and romance from her home in a Cheshire village. She is active in local affairs, and is even called upon to write the script for the annual village pantomime! Her eldest son is a hospital manager, and helps with all her medical research. As part of a close-knit family, she treasures having two of her sons living close by, and the third one not too far away. This also gives her the added pleasure of being able to watch her delightful grandchildren growing up.

Recent titles by the same author:

SWALLOWBROOK'S WINTER BRIDE**
SUMMER SEASIDE WEDDING†
VILLIAGE NURSE'S HAPPY-EVER-AFTER†
WEDDING BELLS FOR THE VILLAGE NURSE†
CHRISTMAS IN BLUEBELL COVE†
COUNTRY MIDWIFE, CHRISTMAS BRIDE*
A SUMMER WEDDING AT WILLOWMERE*
A BABY FOR THE VILLAGE DOCTOR*

***The Doctors of Swallowbrook Farm*
**The Willowmere Village Stories*
†*Bluebell Cove*

CHAPTER ONE

WHEN Hugo Lawrence pulled into the drive of the house where he had lived for the last year and a half on a temporary basis it was a strange feeling to know that it was now his, and that those who had occupied it before had gone on to a new life.

The grey stone detached house, appropriately named Lakes Rise because it was in an elevated position above one of the biggest lakes in the area, had belonged to his widowed sister Patrice and her two young daughters.

Patrice had lost her husband Warren from an undiagnosed heart defect eighteen months previously and stricken with grief had been totally unable to cope, so much so that for the children's sakes as much as anything he had moved from general practice in southern England to take up a similar position in the village of Swallowbrook where she lived, to keep a protective eye on the bereaved family.

Living with them day in day out, comforting and coping as he'd tried to lessen their insecurities and wipe away the tears that the loss of an adored husband and father had brought about had been a gruelling experience and caused him to take a long, hard look at the pain and sorrow that loving too much and too well could cause.

He and his sister had lost their parents when they were in their early teens and as the eldest Hugo had always been very protective of his young sister, often having to put his own life on hold over the years for her sake and never begrudging it.

Patrice's happy marriage had given him five years' respite from that crushing feeling of responsibility towards his sister, and now, with her recent move to Canada, he had begun to breathe easier once again. Not that he begrudged the time he'd spent helping her pick up the pieces, but at least now she had a fresh start to look forward to and he had his own place to start putting down some roots.

When Patrice had talked about putting the house up for sale he had said not to, that he would buy Lakes Rise. He loved the job and got on well with the other two doctors in the practice, *and* it was a very attractive property, but it was the lake nearby, breathtakingly beautiful beneath the towering fells, that attracted so many walkers and climbers and had him spellbound.

Now he couldn't wait to unlock the door, go inside, and celebrate becoming a permanent resident of Swallowbrook with no strings attached.

A shower and a change of clothes, followed by a nice meal with a bottle of wine was what he had promised himself, and after that a good book or watching television. Then maybe to round off the evening a stroll down to The Mallard, the local pub, for a convivial chat with some of the friends he had made since moving here, and finally to bed in the spacious master bedroom of his new home with not a worry on his mind.

But first he wanted to unload the stuff he'd brought with him from his flat down south and stack the bulkier items in the garage for the time being. With that in mind he went round to the back of the car and was opening the boot when a woman's voice hailed him from the bottom of the drive.

Daylight was turning into dusk but when he looked up he could see her beneath the light of a streetlamp. She was tall and slender and appeared to be quite young.

She seemed to be wearing a red cape of sorts with a hood, had black boots with incredibly high heels on her feet, and was holding onto the handle of a large flower-patterned suitcase that she must have been dragging along until she'd stopped on seeing him.

'Could you help me, please?' she asked in a voice so weary he was expecting her to cave in any second. 'Would you happen to know where I can find Libby Gallagher of Lavender Cottage just along the road there? She doesn't appear to be at home, and you are the first person I've seen to ask since getting off the train. Where is everyone?'

'In the process of having their evening meal, I would imagine,' he replied dryly. 'The village will be lively enough later when the locals and visitors gather inside and outside the pub.'

'Please don't mention food,' she groaned, without making any attempt to move closer. 'I'm starving.'

He made his way down the drive towards her. 'Was

Libby expecting you? It isn't like her not to be there if she knew that you were coming.'

'She knows I'm coming back to Swallowbrook and has offered to let me stay with her and her husband until I find somewhere to live, but we hadn't exactly arranged when I was going to arrive.'

'In other words, she wasn't expecting you?'

'Not exactly, no.'

He held back a groan. Libby and Nathan were at their house on the island in the middle of the lake. Since their Christmas wedding the two doctors had gone there every weekend with Toby, Nathan's adopted son.

The three of them loved the place, so he wasn't going to break into their weekend solitude on behalf of this stranger who hadn't bothered to tell them she was coming to join them. She would have to find somewhere to stay for the next two nights…*as far away from him as possible!*

'I know where they are,' he told her stiffly, 'and they won't be back until early Monday morning as they don't like to cut short their weekends for any reason, which means that you are going to have to find somewhere to stay. They have a couple of rooms to let to bed and breakfast visitors at the pub, so I should try there. And now if you'll excuse me…'

As he started to unload the boot it was clear that she wasn't taking the hint. Instead she said, 'It seems as if you know them well, but that's what this place is like, isn't it? Almost everyone is acquainted, or so Libby tells me.'

Hugo sighed. He wasn't in the mood for small talk,

but at least he could be polite and in answer to her first comment. He said, 'Yes, I know Libby and Nathan very well. My name is Hugo Lawrence. I'm a GP too and work with them both at the practice.'

'Oh, well, then, you might have heard them mention me,' she said slowly. 'I'm Ruby Hollister, shortly to join you all there as a trainee GP.'

Hugo looked her over once more and frowned. Surely this couldn't possibly be the girl that Libby and Nathan had been so keen to have as part of the medical team at the surgery, who had got a first at one of the top medical colleges in the country.

There had been a few practice meetings of late about taking on another doctor as Libby was pregnant and intending doing fewer hours at the practice in the near future, prior to becoming a stay-at-home wife and mother to Toby and the baby, when it came.

Apparently Ruby Hollister had lived in the village with her parents until her teens and then they'd moved away, but like Libby she had always had leanings towards practising medicine amongst the lakes and fells.

'Ah, now I understand,' he said, gathering his wits fast. 'I knew that you were about to join us, but was away all last week and wasn't aware that it was to be so soon.'

She was leaning on the case. He could see weariness in the droop of her shoulders and knowing that he couldn't just send her off to the pub to find accommodation now that he knew who she was, he pointed to the house and said reluctantly, 'I think you had better come inside while we sort out where you are going to stay until Libby and Nathan come home from their weekend away.'

'You're very kind,' she said meekly, and removing the case from her grasp he took charge of it with one hand, unlocked the door with the other, and ushered her into the sitting room where at his invitation she perched on the edge of a nearby sofa and looked around her listlessly.

Why she was so weary he had no idea, but he knew complete exhaustion when he saw it and he was seeing it now. Waving goodbye to his evening of joyful relaxation, he asked, 'Which would you prefer, a brandy or a cup of hot, sweet tea?'

'Tea would be lovely, thanks,' she replied, fixing him with huge brown eyes, 'and I could really go for a slice of toast if you have any bread in the house after being away.'

'I think I could just about manage that,' he said dryly, far from thrilled at the prospect of entertaining his newest colleague all evening.

But when he appeared with the tea and toast it was to find her asleep, huddled against the cushions still in the red cape, and with the high-heeled boots placed neatly on the carpet beside her.

He went upstairs and taking a blanket out of the linen cupboard on the landing covered her with it from head to toe, then went to make the meal he had promised himself, with an extra portion for his unexpected guest when she woke up. When he'd finished eating he went to sit across from her with a book.

Why had she arrived so unexpectedly like this? he

wondered as he watched her sleeping soundly beneath the blanket. Obviously she had made some arrangement with Libby and not kept to it, because as head of the practice Libby would not have gone away for the weekend if she'd known that Ruby was arriving today.

The minutes ticked by and she still slept. As ten o'clock drew near Hugo thought there was still time to check if they had a room vacant for a couple of nights at The Mallard. He would willingly cover the cost if they had in order to retrieve the privacy that he'd been so looking forward to. But there was no way he could rouse this girl into wakefulness and bundle her out of his house into strange surroundings for the night.

As ten o'clock came and went he picked her up into his arms, carried her upstairs, and laid her gently on the top of his bed still wrapped in the blanket, with the thought uppermost that at least she would be safe there with him dozing downstairs and everywhere locked and bolted.

He awoke with a crick in his neck and a dry mouth in a pale winter dawn and his first thought was about the woman upstairs. Was she still sleeping or had he dreamt that she had descended upon him from out of nowhere and ruined his first night of peaceful living?

The clatter of dishes in the kitchen told him he hadn't been dreaming and when he went to investigate she was brewing a pot of tea and making toast.

As he stood framed in the doorway she swung round to face him. 'I am so sorry for being such a nuisance last night, Dr Lawrence. I'd had a really dreadful day and was foolish enough to take it for granted that Libby and Nathan would be here when I arrived.'

Slumping down onto a kitchen chair, she explained. 'I'd given up the flat that I'd been renting while at college in readiness for moving to Swallowbrook and had been staying with a friend. Early yesterday morning I had a hospital appointment and had a long wait to see the consultant. As I was driving back to where I was staying my car broke down. Breakdown services had to come out to it and they towed it away, all of which was stressful enough, but that wasn't all.

'When I returned to the place where I was staying I discovered that my so-called friend had let someone else take my place in the flat and I had no choice but to gather my belongings together and face the fact that I was homeless.

'The solution seemed to be to come straight here instead of in two weeks' time as had been arranged, but having no car I had to seek out a train and had to wait hours for one to bring me to Swallowbrook, and by then I was wilting badly. I know it was crazy not to check that Libby and Nathan would be here, but in my semi-deranged state I took it for granted that they would be. So now you know why I was wandering about like a lost soul when I saw you pull up here.

'So if you will bear with me for a little longer while I have a drink and a bite,' she was saying, 'I will look around for somewhere to stay for the rest of the weekend and leave you in peace in your beautiful house. How long have you lived here?'

'Almost two years as a visitor and just the one week

since it became legally mine. It was my sister's house and I bought it off her when she went to live abroad.

'I'm sorry that yesterday turned out to be so dreadful for you. I do hope that nothing connected with your hospital visit combined to make it even more traumatic.' Before she could reply to that he went on, 'With regard to your car being out of action we do have a spare vehicle at the surgery that you will be able to use until it has been repaired.'

With the feeling that he'd said enough in a conciliatory manner he poured himself a cup of tea, buttered a slice of toast, and as silence fell between them seated himself opposite.

How could he be so cool, calm and collected? wondered Ruby. It was clear that one of the most attractive men she'd met in years was anxious to see her gone and could she blame him? She'd slept in her clothes and looked a mess. Had flaked out on his sofa and let him carry her upstairs without even being aware of it, *and* she squirmed every time she thought about the look on his face when he'd realised that she was going to be the new doctor at the surgery.

His house was gorgeous and so was he. It seemed as if he lived there alone, which could mean anything. That he was divorced, was too choosy, or maybe played the field. Whatever was going on in his life he wasn't exactly a bundle of laughs, that was for sure, but, then, who would be after giving up his bed for the night to some strange woman?

He was tall. She was no midget, but he towered above

her and he was trim with it. His eyes were blue as a summer sky, his hair a much darker thatch than her chestnut mane, and he had the most kissable mouth.

It would seem that she was going to be seeing a lot of him in days to come, which was almost enough to make up for the traumas of yesterday, but not quite. Medicine was the love of *her* life, it had to be. As well as being good at it, she needed it to fill the gap that a fluke of nature was to blame for.

She'd come top out of all the students on her course, but wasn't going to be bandying that item of news around the Swallowbrook surgery. Anyone hearing it would be sure to want to know why, if that was the case, she was prepared to vegetate in a Lakeland village practice.

There *was* a reason, a sentimental one. In her early teens she and her family had been on the point of leaving Swallowbrook to move up north because of her father's job when her baby brother had been taken seriously ill, and it had been the prompt action of the head of the practice at that time that had saved his life.

In her conversations with Libby Gallagher regarding the job Ruby had learned that Libby's father-in-law, John Gallagher, who had been there for Robbie in their time of need, was now retired, and that she and her husband had taken over his father's practice.

Her family's move away had been urgent, her father's job had depended on it, and no sooner had her young brother's illness been stabilised than they'd been on their way, but she had never forgotten what the Swallowbrook practice had done for Robbie. On leaving the village she'd told Dr Gallagher that one day she was going to come back to be one of them and now her dream was about to come true.

Nathan had remembered her vaguely from long ago, the teenage kid who'd wanted to be one of them some day, and when she'd got in touch with the news that she'd got a first she'd been offered her heart's desire, a position in the practice, and now here she was, ready to burst upon the Swallowbrook medical scene, in a strange man's house and looking an absolute mess.

He couldn't just throw her out in the hope that the pub might have a spare room for tonight , thought Hugo. It was barely half past eight on a Sunday morning. Apart from the bellringers in the church tower reminding those who would listen that it was the Sabbath, all was still, nothing moved.

How was Ruby going to pass the time on a chilly spring day with nowhere to stay, and Libby and Nathan unaware that their protégé had arrived unexpectedly?

There was the apartment above the double garage, of course. If she hadn't fallen into such a deep sleep the night before he might have mentioned it then. He could offer her the use of it until tomorrow and it would serve a dual purpose from his point of view. Ease his conscience with regard to wanting her out of his space and give him peace of mind knowing that he hadn't turned her out without accommodation.

Before it had been turned into an apartment the area above the garage had been a study and sitting room that his late brother-in-law had used, and when she had lost him one of the few decisive things that Patrice had done was to have the accommodation made into a small apartment for letting to help out financially. It was usually occupied by visitors to the lakes from Easter onwards but as it was out of season it was currently empty.

Ruby was observing his expression and wondering what was coming next. The feeling that she was ruining his weekend was heavy in the air and she certainly was not expecting a suggestion as welcome as the one he was about to make.

'There is a self-contained apartment above the garage.' he told her. 'You can use that until tomorrow if you wish. No need to go looking for somewhere to stay. There's plenty of food in my fridge and freezer so just help yourself to what you want if you would like to make use of the accommodation.'

The generosity of the offer made her want to weep. The last thing she'd been looking forward to was trudging around the village with her flowery suitcase.

'That would be fantastic,' she told him gratefully. 'If there is a bath I can have a nice long soak to take away the stresses of yesterday.'

'Yes, of course there is a bathroom,' he said dryly, 'and now, if you will excuse me, I heard the Sunday papers drop through the letter box a few moments ago and am going to bring myself up to date with what is going on in the world.'

He paused in the kitchen doorway and as if he hadn't been dismissive enough said, 'Let me know when you want to go across there and I'll take you on a short guided tour.'

'I'm ready now,' she said meekly, eager to take advantage of his reluctant hospitality.

'OK. So go and sort out what food you want to take with you and I'll bring your case down. The sooner you're settled in there the better you'll feel, even though it will only be for the one night.'

And the happier you will be on both counts she thought. Count one because it is only for one night, and count two because you will have your privacy back, but you will still have to endure my presence at the surgery Dr Lawrence, and you could be in for a surprise as my sparkle has only been dimmed, not extinguished.

'Oh! This is lovely,' she said, looking around her at the pristine open-plan dining room and kitchen. Her glance went to the window. 'I can see the lake through the trees!'

Hugo was checking that the lighting and central heating were switched on at the mains and didn't reply. He just nodded his agreement and pointed towards the apartment's one bedroom and en suite arrangements for her to inspect.

'I hope I'll be able to find somewhere like this when I start looking for accommodation next week,' she said wistfully, and waited to see if he would rise to the implied suggestion, but it fell on stony ground and once he had satisfied himself that she was au fait with the workings of everything he said, 'Libby and Nathan usually get back from their weekends away around half past seven on a Monday morning, so you should be able to get in touch with them tomorrow any time after that.

'If you should leave here after I've gone to the surgery just drop the keys through my letter box.' And off he went…to read the Sunday papers while she did some unpacking and had that long soak that she had promised herself.

Then, after making a meal of sorts from the food that Hugo had insisted she take with her, she changed into jeans and a thick sweater and went to renew her acquaintance with the stretch of water that was as familiar to her as her own face, taking care not to pass his windows on the way as the feeling that the dishy though unwelcoming Dr Lawrence had seen enough of her to be going on with was getting stronger by the minute.

But the moment she reached the lakeside he was forgotten in the pleasure of watching a launch go by on its calm waters and the sight of the sails of yachts gleaming whitely against the rugged sweep of the fells, the ageless guardians of the valley.

It felt so right to be back where she had made her promise to the Swallowbrook practice. The only blot on the horizon was the taciturn Dr Lawrence, who hadn't been able to get her out of his orbit quickly enough. If she'd had any grandiose ideas about herself they would have disappeared completely at the thought of having to compete with the Sunday papers for his attention.

She went to The Mallard for her evening meal as several hours of her own company was beginning to pall and once she was installed in the dining room amongst the friendly chatter of its patrons the feeling of loneliness that was tugging at her began to disappear.

Until during the last hour before the place was due to close her reluctant host appeared and his eyes widened at the vision of her seated beside the big log fire that was one of the main features of the place.

The sight of him brought Ruby to her feet. She was ready to leave immediately as if caught doing something he wouldn't approve of. As she wished him a meek goodnight and tried to pass him in the crowded room Hugo said, 'If you're going back to the apartment I'll walk along with you.' When she was about to protest at being singled out in front of everyone, he added, 'Please don't object. It isn't good that you should be out alone at such a late hour.'

She didn't reply, just continued making her way towards the door, and as he followed he was remembering how flat his evening had been until now. After shunting Ruby out to the apartment above the garage he had expected his joy at his longed-for return to normality to clock in, but instead of that he hadn't been able to settle.

And now, instead of livening himself up with a last drink of the day with friends and acquaintances, he was fussing once again over this young woman who probably thought nothing of being out all night on her own, let alone walking just the short distance to where she'd been accommodated for the night.

They walked the first few yards along the road in silence and then, ashamed of her irritation at his concern for her, Ruby said, 'I walked by the lake this afternoon and it was so lovely to be back. Do you go down there much?'

It sounded trite, but she couldn't think of anything else to say and he was actually smiling when he replied, 'It is the lake that has made me want to stay in Swallowbrook instead of going back down south to practice. Did you remember the house on the island from when you once lived here?

'That is where Libby, Nathan, and their son spend their weekends. Here in the village they have cottages next to each other and now they are married are having the two made into one big one for weekdays. Otherwise I suppose you could have stayed in the empty one.'

'I'll find somewhere, even if it means sleeping on a park bench or in an empty boat house,' she assured him breezily as another reminder had come her way to the effect that where she was going to live was only his problem for a few more hours.

With Lakes Rise and the apartment only feet away, she said in a more restrained manner, 'Thank you for your company once more Dr Lawrence. You are very kind. What will you do now? Go back to The Mallard for what is left of the evening?'

'Possibly,' he told her, keen to let her know subtly that he wasn't always going to be at her beck and call.

CHAPTER TWO

MAKING his way back to the light and noise of The Mallard, Hugo was feeling uncomfortable about the way Ruby had risen to her feet and prepared to leave the moment he'd appeared, as if keen to avoid any further contact.

He'd noticed immediately that the red cape had been discarded for the time being and that dressed in dark blue jeans, a short white jacket and wearing flat walking shoes she looked smaller than when she'd been wobbling on high heels the day before.

She was attractive in a pale, ethereal sort of way, he'd decided as she'd been making her way through the crowded room towards the exit, and the thought had crossed his mind that the life of the GP was not always easy—would a person as vulnerable looking as Ruby be up to it?

With his determination still in place to stay aloof, he hadn't lingered when they'd arrived back at the house and now that was also niggling at him. Ruby hadn't put a foot wrong since interrupting the free time that he'd been so looking forward to, yet he was treating her as if she had the plague.

The thought of going back to have a drink with friends was losing its appeal so, turning, he retraced his steps and when Lakes Rise appeared once more he noted that the apartment was in darkness. After checking that it was secure from all angles, he opened his own front door and went inside.

Lying wide awake up above, Ruby had heard him try the door and thought that with any other man she might have wondered as to his motive, but not Hugo Lawrence. He wouldn't have any plans to join her, like some predatory types might think of doing.

The dishy doctor would be satisfying himself that *she* wasn't intending seeking *him* out again before morning, as he'd made it clear that in spite of looking after the basics of her wellbeing he wanted his privacy back as soon as possible.

Perhaps at some time in the future when she'd got to know him better, and that would have to happen no matter what, with them both working at the practice, she would suggest that The Hermitage would be a better name than Lakes Rise for his beautiful house and see if Hugo thought that as hilarious as she did.

But there were other things on her mind, much more important than her reluctant host. During the trauma of yesterday and her subsequent extreme weariness she'd put to the back of her mind what the haematology department had said during her check-up at the hospital in the town where she'd been based all the time she'd been studying for her degree.

It had been nothing new, she'd had the same discussion with similar departments of the NHS that were geared to her potential problem and nothing had happened to make her change her decision.

But it was still nonetheless heartbreaking because she had to face up to it and accept it for the rest of her life. She wouldn't be able to live with herself if she didn't. But one day the test would come and what would she do then?

Putting aside memories of the punishing past, she reminded herself that tomorrow she would be starting an exciting new life as a doctor in the Swallowbrook Farm Medical Practice, something she had promised herself she was going to do long ago, and maybe the pains and hurts of that other time would seem less if she could make her mark in the medical centre that had served her family so well in their time of need, and with that thought the painful memories came crowding back.

Robbie had been just a toddler and she'd been fourteen when the nightmare had begun and changed their lives for ever. The family had been on the point of leaving Swallowbrook to move to Tyneside, where her father's job was taking them, when Robbie had had his first bleed and it had been action stations on Dr John Gallagher's part without a moment to spare when it had happened. She'd crouched in fear and trembling by his hospital bed, wondering what it was all about, while her frantic parents had tried to cope with the mention of haemophilia, the hereditary bleeding disease, being present in the family.

Their move had been imminent yet she hadn't wanted to move away from Swallowbrook, she'd felt safe there, but the arrangements had still had to go ahead or her father might have lost his job, so even while they had been waiting for the results from Robbie's tests they had left the village with arrangements in place that the findings would be transferred to the haematology department at a hospital near their new home.

The results had been positive. The lack of a clotting agent in Robbie's blood had caused the serious bleed. He had inherited the problem from their mother who unknown to her was a carrier of the faulty gene that caused the condition.

The hospital had explained that hereditary illnesses had to start somewhere and the reason their mother hadn't known about it was because she was the first one in her family who had ever been a known carrier of the haemophilia gene.

Now Robbie was twelve, and medically much better cared for, due to new treatments, than past sufferers, but the anxiety was always there for his parents and big sister, who had been left with anxieties of her own to cope with.

She fell asleep at last, too tired to think anymore about the ups and downs in her life, and awoke the next morning to a room filled with pale sunshine and the sound of the engines of one of the large launches that crossed the lake at regular intervals chugging its way across its smooth surface.

It has arrived, she thought excitedly, hugging herself with delight. She was back in her dream village, about to start her dream job.

* * *

Hugo's thoughts were running along very different lines when he surfaced in the big bedroom that he'd carried Ruby up to the night before last. Thoughts of her consumed him now, how could they not whilst she was his temporary tenant and soon-to-be colleague? It seemed she was sorted for work, but just what did she plan to do for accommodation?

So far he'd had no bookings for the apartment over the garage, as requests for accommodation around the lakes didn't usually commence until nearer Easter. So why shouldn't he offer to rent it to her long term if she was interested?

She'd certainly seemed impressed on her first viewing of it, which was not surprising as it was a delightful small let, and for someone like her who was probably having to carry the burden of repaying a student loan, he could afford to be generous in what he asked for rental, just as long as she stayed on her side of their living arrangements, and left him to enjoy his well-earned rest with an easy conscience after having helped her to settle back into the village to some small degree.

He'd known that a medical graduate was joining them in a couple of weeks. That she'd lived in the village when she was young and even then had wanted to be part of the practice when she grew up.

Along with his two partners he had been in favour of taking a talented young newcomer into the practice to help cope with their growing number of patients as new lakeside properties were being built all the time, and had agreed that she would help to fill the gap that

would be coming soon when Libby wanted to point herself towards full-time motherhood.

He was pretty sure that she and Nathan would be
surprised when they discovered that the newcomer
had arrived earlier than expected, but would be better
equipped to deal with it than he'd been.

It wasn't so much her sudden appearance as the way
he'd coped with it that was making him feel uncomfortable, but the offer of the accommodation above the
garage should hopefully redeem him!

When he got up from the breakfast table Hugo
glanced down the road as he often did to where the
lake could be seen a short distance away with the fells
towering above it, and the feeling of rightness that it
always gave him was there, until he saw a slender figure wearing a red cape over a neat grey dress striding
briskly towards the house with pale cheeks rosy from
the winter morning's chill and hair fastened back off
her face into a neat twist.

She was moving straight towards the apartment without a glance in his direction but when he opened his
front door and called across to her she came slowly towards him.

'You're up bright and early,' he commented when
they came face to face. 'The surgery won't be open for
another hour.'

'Yes, I know,' she told him, 'I've been down by the
lake again and stopped for a coffee at the only café that
was open at this time.'

'I wanted a word,' he said, stepping back to let her

into the hallway. She entered hesitantly. 'I've been having a think about your accommodation problem.'

He saw surprise in the big brown eyes observing him for a second and then it was replaced by wariness. She didn't speak, just waited to hear what he had to say, and as she listened she was filled with delighted amazement.

'If you should feel that you would like to rent the apartment I would be willing to discuss it with you,' he was saying. 'On thinking about it I feel that it would be easier from my point of view to have just one regular tenant in there, rather than having to deal with different ones all the time on a holiday let basis.

'So think about it, and if you are interested let me know, but before you do I feel that I must tell you that at this time of year there are always lots of places to rent before the holiday season clocks in. So feel free to use the apartment for the time being until you've had time to sort out your priorities with Libby and Nathan, as they might already have somewhere in mind for you.'

She was dumbstruck. Of course she would want to stay in the lovely apartment where she'd spent the night, but what had changed? Only yesterday she'd felt that Hugo Lawrence was irritated by her presence, keen to see the back of her, and now...?

Concealing her pleasure at the thought of accepting his offer, she answered gravely, 'I will do as you say, Dr Lawrence, and give your suggestion some thought. Thank you for allowing me to stay until I have had the chance to do that, and now if you will excuse me I'm going to have some breakfast before presenting myself at the surgery.'

'Sure,' he agreed easily. 'I'll see you there later. I hope that your first day will be a good one.'

Once inside the apartment Ruby's gravity was cast aside and she danced around the place delightedly. Of course she was going to take up Hugo Lawrence's offer, but after the way she'd butted into his well-organised life and been received with what could only be described as reluctance, a more staid approach was called for when she was in his company.

As for the rest of it, she was in a state of bliss at his suggestion because the surgery *and the lake* were so close. She would be able to explore all her old haunts again. Life was as good as it was likely to get, just as long as the precarious path to good health that her young brother had to travel along didn't have any life-threatening side turnings.

Hugo was smiling when she'd gone. Not so docile this morning, was she? It would be interesting to see how she came over at the practice with Libby, Nathan, the rest of the staff *and the patients*. Maybe he should have offered to drive her down there instead of leaving her to make a solo appearance, but he wanted to call on one of his patients who was causing grave concern on his way to the surgery, and in any case the newcomer needed to stand on her own two feet from the start.

'Ruby! Is it really you?' Libby exclaimed as she was opening up the surgery at eight o'clock and saw the new junior doctor approaching.

'We were not expecting you just yet.'

'I know,' Ruby told her apologetically. 'But I suddenly found myself homeless on Saturday and decided
that the only thing to do was come straight here and
hope you wouldn't mind me descending upon you without notice.'

'And we weren't here, were we? What a shame! So
where have you stayed for the last two days?' Libby
asked, and taking her arm, 'Come inside out of the cold
and we'll have a cup of tea and a chat before everyone
arrives. Nathan is at the cottage, getting Toby ready for
school, and will be here about half past nine when he's
seen him safely inside.'

'I hope you don't mind me arriving too soon,' Ruby
said as Libby brewed a pot of tea in a pleasant kitchen
at the far end of the building.

'Not at all,' she assured her. 'We are very busy and
badly need your input in the practice, but I haven't yet
sorted out anywhere for you to live, so we must see to
that before anything else.'

The young newcomer was smiling. 'I'm already fixed
up with accommodation. When I arrived on Saturday
in a pretty distressed state I asked the first person I saw
if he knew where you might be and it turned out that I
was speaking to Dr Lawrence.'

She wasn't going to mention sleeping in his room on
top of his bed! 'He let me use the apartment over his
garage until now, and has said if I want to rent it I can.'

'You've already met Hugo, then!' Libby exclaimed,
'and he's willing to let you rent that delightful apartment! Wow! You must have made a good impression.'

'I doubt it,' she said whimsically, 'but I think he feels

that a regular tenant is the lesser of two evils rather than one let after another. He's told me to think about it, not to rush into anything I might regret, but I don't need to, the place is gorgeous so I'm going to agree to his suggestion before he changes his mind.'

The rest of the staff was arriving in ones and twos and as she was introduced to each in turn Ruby's dream was being realised. When at last she and Libby were alone in the small consulting room that would be hers she said, 'I'm so grateful for this opportunity to be part of the Swallowbrook practice, Dr Gallagher.'

'And we are delighted to have you with us,' Libby told her. 'If there is anything that you're not sure of don't be afraid to ask.' As Nathan appeared at that moment to offer his words of welcome, she said to him, 'Ruby has already met Hugo. He took her in for the weekend when we weren't around and has offered her the apartment above his garage to rent.'

'Really!' he exclaimed laughingly. 'That doesn't exactly fit in with his expressed desire for no visitors and time to himself when away from this place. You are to be congratulated, Ruby.'

She smiled. It was hardly the moment to explain that he had accommodated her on sufferance…and where was he? Hugo Lawrence didn't strike her as someone who would be a poor timekeeper.

The two doctors had left her to settle into her room and gone to deal with their patients, when there was a knock on the door. She crossed to open it and there he was, in the passage outside, observing her questioningly.

'Is everything all right?' he asked before she had the chance to greet him. 'You've met Libby and Nathan and the rest of the staff?'

'Yes, everything is fine,' she said brightly. 'Libby was concerned because she hadn't had time to find me somewhere to stay with me arriving earlier than expected, but I told her that I'd already had a very good offer of your apartment that I will be delighted to accept if it is still open.'

He was frowning. 'When you get to know me better, Ruby, you will discover that I usually mean what I say. So, yes, the apartment is yours for a nominal rent for as long as you want. If you will come across to the house this evening, we'll sort out the details.

'Now, if you'll excuse me, I must ring the hospital to have a patient admitted who is far from well with what appears to be septicaemia. Last week it was a mild infection that could have gone either way, but I've just called at the house and his condition has worsened over the weekend into something quite serious.'

'Will you have time to tell me about it when you've made the call?' she asked.

'Er, maybe not at the moment as I have patients waiting, but if you're still keen to know I'll tell you about it tonight when you come round to discuss your renting of the apartment.' he replied. 'So, what have Libby and Nathan got planned for you on your first day here?'

He could have suggested that Ruby sit in with him during his consultations for today, but wasn't going to as he felt he'd made enough concessions already towards welcoming her into the fold, and maybe she would be better sitting in with Libby on her first morning at the practice.

As if on cue Libby appeared and said, 'I thought you might like to join me during my consultations today, Ruby. It will give you the feel of things and an insight as to how and what we have to deal with, don't you agree, Hugo?'

'Yes, I do,' he told her, 'and I have an urgent phone call to make so I'll leave you both to it.' And with a smile that embraced them both he strode off to his own particular part of the busy surgery, while Libby did likewise in the direction of hers with Ruby close behind.

It had been a fantastic day, reflected Ruby as she ate her solitary meal that evening. Even Dr Lawrence had had a smile for her and soon she would be seeing him again when she went to discuss the rental procedures, and he satisfied her eagerness to hear about the infection that he'd been dealing with.

But first she was going to ring home. She'd spoken to Robbie and her parents yesterday, so they were aware that she had arrived in Swallowbrook earlier than expected, and would now be waiting to hear how her first day at the practice had gone.

They were a close-knit family and had been a very happy one until Robbie's illness had shown itself and her mother had been faced with the dreadful impact of her part in it.

Before she'd discovered that she had the faulty gene she'd always been happy and carefree, singing around the house, hugging them all close at every opportunity, but ever since Robbie had been stricken with that first bleed all that time ago and had had others since, she had become quiet and withdrawn, not loving or caring for them any less, more if that were possible but joyless in the process.

As Ruby had grown older and begun her medical career she had understood more than anyone the feeling of being flawed that was with her mother constantly and once when she'd asked her what she would have done if she'd known she carried the gene, she'd replied sadly, 'I don't know, Ruby. Because I didn't know I was a carrier of the haemophilia gene I was never faced with having to make a choice with regard to having children.

'Your dad is loving and supportive, tells me to stop fretting, that I am not to blame for what is happening to Robbie, that it is not because of any known fault of mine, genetics have made me what I am, but I still have to live with it, don't I? Live with the knowledge that Robbie's illness isn't the only blight I've put upon my family. There is also what I've done to you, Ruby.'

On that occasion with a wisdom beyond her years she had held her mother close and told her, 'All you've ever *done* to me is to be the best mother in the world and Robbie, when he is older, will feel the same, so don't weep for what you didn't know about, Mum. What Dad says is right.'

But tonight when her mother's voice came over the line there was only happiness in it as they chatted about Ruby's return to Swallowbrook and her first day at the practice, until she told her about her attractive landlord-cum-colleague-cum–recluse neighbour.

'You aren't going to fall in love, are you?' her mother asked, trying not to sound anxious.

They'd gone through this scenario a few times, the worry that relationships with the opposite sex brought about, and understanding only too well her mother's thought process Ruby told her gently, 'Not with this one. He is dubious about my suitability from all angles.'

When she'd finished speaking to her mother Ruby rang Hugo to ask what time he would like her to go across to the house to discuss the tenancy.

'Come now if you want and let's get it over with,' was the brisk reply, without any hint of welcome. 'It won't take long. Just a matter of fixing a rental, the two of us signing the appropriate forms, and me giving you a copy of rules and regulations, along with details of the user instructions for everything.'

So 'Mr Nice Guy' from the surgery had changed back into 'Sir Keep Your Distance', Ruby thought as she replaced the receiver. What did he think she was going to do, take her knitting with her? She would be in and out like a flash and would not be asking him to tell her about the patient that he'd called to see on his way to the surgery that morning.

She wasn't to know that he'd been expecting a call from his sister, and as always when he spoke to Patrice there was the dread in him that the new life she'd gone to without a second thought might turn out to be a mistake.

When she'd gone it had been as if he'd been given his life back. Opportunities to do his own thing for a change had presented themselves and he was out to guard them like precious gold.

Patrice always rang him on a Monday evening and until she did he was always on edge in case she was having second thoughts about her impulsive move abroad and wanted to come home. So far there had been no mention of any such thing, she and the children sounded happy enough in their new surroundings, but so stressful had been the eighteen months when he'd given up every spare moment to them he still couldn't believe that it was actually over and she had found some degree of happiness at last.

He'd thought it was going to be her when Ruby had phoned. Had let his tension loose on her and was now regretting it, so when he opened the door to her he was smiling. Stepping back to let her in, he said, 'My sister usually rings from Canada at this time on a Monday evening, so I hope you will excuse me if I have to break into our discussion to answer the call. I am always on edge until I know that all is well with her—you know how it can be, a new life in a new land.'

'Yes, of course,' she replied, and thought she would bear in mind that Monday evenings were not a good time to ring her prospective landlord.

He was leading her through to the sitting room and pointing to the sofa for her to be seated and the memory of Saturday night came back, with her drooping like a rag doll against its soft cushions after a dreadful day.

Hugo had been right when he'd said that the rental

arrangements wouldn't take long. In no time at all they had completed the paperwork needed for Ruby to rent the apartment for the next six months, to begin with at a very reasonable figure.

When she expressed her gratitude he said with none of the abruptness of earlier, 'I thought you might have to pay off a student loan, and it is worth it to me that someone I already know will be living there, instead of an array of strangers.'

'I do have a loan to pay off,' she told him. 'My parents are helping me with it, yet it is still my responsibility, so thanks for the thought, Dr Lawrence.'

He nodded and asked with casual curiosity, 'Where is your family situated?'

'In Tyneside. We used to live here in Swallowbrook but had to move because of my father's job, yet I have always wanted to come back.'

'Are you their only child?'

'No, I have a young brother, Robbie, in his early teens.'

'So your parents have the same as mine had, a son and a daughter, though in our family it is the other way round—my sister, Patrice, is the younger of the two of us.'

At that moment the phone rang and he said, 'This will be her now.'

As she got up to go he said, 'You don't have to rush off. I thought you wanted to hear about the patient I called on before morning surgery.'

She was smiling, her earlier dismay at his abrupt manner having disappeared as she said, 'It will keep

for another time,' and letting herself out she returned
to the apartment and once again danced a little jig at
the thought of being its new tenant.

CHAPTER THREE

THE CURTAINS were not drawn in the apartment and as Hugo chatted to Patrice he was smiling as he watched Ruby dancing around the place.

She was incredibly graceful, he thought as she pirouetted in the small lounge beneath the chandelier that had been one of his sister's extravagances when she'd been furnishing the elegant apartment.

Now Patrice was gone. It belonged to him, and it remained to be seen what kind of a person the young graduate that he had rented it to would turn out to be. So far she hadn't put a foot wrong, *but he had*, and there had been no reason for it except that the timing of her arrival in his life had been all wrong.

Looking after Patrice had become a way of life over the years and since it had come to an end, every time they spoke on the phone he rejoiced to hear the lift in her voice as she chatted about the children's schools, and the attractive house they'd moved into not far away from that of her friend.

When they'd finished their weekly chat he saw that Ruby had closed the curtains across the way and settling himself in a chair by the fire with a book he thought that he wouldn't be doing this tomorrow night as Libby and Nathan had invited him to supper, along with Ruby and John Gallagher, who was now enjoying his retirement in a pine lodge by the side of a nearby river.

Ruby hadn't mentioned the invitation when she'd come across, but she hadn't had much opportunity with him wanting to know about her family and anything else that would give him a clearer picture of the newcomer to the practice, and then there had been Patrice's phone call.

It was a nice idea on the part of the other two doctors. Ruby's early arrival had taken them all by surprise. It would be one way of welcoming her into their midst, and an opportunity for her to meet up again with John, who had been her family's doctor when she'd lived in Swallowbrook before.

Not having been resident here for long himself, he knew nothing of the trauma of illness and heartache that Ruby's family had taken with them to their new home. What he did know was that she had been very keen to come back to Swallowbrook to be part of the village medical centre, which was rather strange as with her degree results he would have thought she would want to aim higher than a country practice.

The book he was holding was in his hand without a word having been read and deciding that solitude was all right in small doses he reached for a jacket and going out into the night pointed himself in the direction of The Mallard, and this time there was no Ruby rising hastily from her seat by the fire to make a quick exit.

* * *

Having calmed down after her earlier glee at the thought of securing the apartment, Ruby was towelling herself dry in front of a large mirror in the bathroom after her nightly luxurious bath when catching sight of herself she paused in contemplation.

There was nothing wrong with her figure, she thought wistfully, slender curves, smooth skin, and long legs that made up for any raving beauty that was missing elsewhere. But it wasn't anything that was *missing* that frequently made her feel sad, just the opposite. It was something she had that she didn't want, that might one day turn light into darkness.

Don't let it spoil the pleasure of being back here, she told herself.

Soon it would be spring and everywhere would come alive as it always had before. The lake would be filled with launches and small boats and the fells would be beckoning the climbers and walkers who couldn't resist them onto their rugged slopes. But best of all there would be the practice and knowing that she was back in the place that had wrapped itself around her and held her close when her world had fallen apart.

When she came out of the apartment the next morning Hugo was about to pull out of the drive and he wound the car window down to ask if she wanted a lift to the surgery.

She flashed him a smile but shook her head, 'No. I'm fine, thank you, Dr Lawrence. I'm still in a state of delight to be back here and will enjoy the short walk.'

It was true she would, but the main reason she'd refused the lift was because she didn't want Hugo Lawrence to feel that his reluctant overseeing of her welfare had to continue.

She was up and running, ready for any challenge that came her way in the new life she had chosen for herself, just as long as she could put on hold the interest he had awakened in her from the moment of their meeting.

About to drive off, he said as a parting comment, 'We'll have to sort out you taking over the spare car at the surgery that I mentioned. Can't have you without transport, even though you do enjoy walking everywhere.'

'Yes, when you're ready,' she agreed obediently, and off he went.

Hugo's face was set in solemn lines as he pulled up on the forecourt of the practice. What was the matter with him, he was thinking, fussing over this young doctor to such a degree? Had the time he'd spent looking after the needs of his sister and her children turned him into a control freak? The void he'd lived in for the last eighteen months was opening up and life was going to be good again, if he would let it.

If Ruby Hollister had turned up smartly dressed and brimming with confidence on Saturday he wouldn't have given her a second thought, but it was as if she'd appeared in his life for a reason, and of one thing he was sure, it was not going to be as someone to fill the gap.

She could sort herself out in future. He would keep

his distance, and no sooner had that determination been born than he remembered the supper party at Libby and Nathan's that evening.

Unaware of his thought processes, Ruby sought him out before the morning got under way and said, 'I'm on my own today with instructions to ask any of the three of you if I have any problems, but as I'm sure that you must feel you've already seen enough of *me and my problems* I'll avoid troubling you further and will consult either Libby or Nathan.'

'Sure,' he said easily. 'Whatever you're happy with, Ruby, and by the way, do you still want to know about the patient with septicaemia?'

'Yes, of course,' she said promptly. 'I want to know about everything and everyone in this place.' And into the silence that followed came the thought, *You in particular.*

'Right, then,' he said briskly. 'Jeremy Jones is the village postman and I have never seen an infection develop more quickly than the one he's got. He was sawing up wood for the open fire in his cottage with a rusty saw and it slipped and gashed his leg quite badly.

'Instead of getting it seen to in a proper manner to prevent any complications, he has been bathing it with all sorts of old remedies, typical of an elderly bachelor who thought he knew best, and didn't.

'He called me out last Friday and I put him on antibiotics immediately with instructions to call out the emergency services over the weekend if it worsened before the medication had a chance to kick in and the dreaded red line of septicaemia appeared.

'Jeremy decided to wait until Monday morning when one of us was available, but before he could get in touch I called to see him on my way here, if you remember, and from then on it was all systems go to get him into hospital. I'm afraid that he might lose the leg through nothing more than his own negligence as he hadn't taken the medication I'd prescribed.'

'How could he have been so foolish with all the facilities of the NHS at his disposal?' she exclaimed.

'Yes, exactly,' he agreed, and as the big hand of the surgery clock swung on to half past eight Ruby went into her own small room and picking up a patient's notes from the top of a small pile on the desk went to find him.

There were a few surprised glances when she appeared in the doorway of the waiting room and as she smiled upon them she wondered how many of them would shy away from consulting a doctor of her obvious youthfulness.

But the spotty teenage youth who got to his feet in answer to his name didn't care who he was being seen by as long as they could do something to put an end to the misery that a face covered in pimples was causing him.

'I've come about these zits,' he said awkwardly. 'I can't face going anywhere with my skin like this and I don't know what to do about it.'

Ruby flashed him a friendly smile. 'Maybe you don't,

Dominic, but I do. You've come to the right place. It is acne that you've got, the teenage blight.

'It will have started by blackheads appearing, am I right?' He nodded sombrely. 'Then the blackheads became zits, and if those zits aren't treated they will become cysts that are infected with bacteria made up of dead skin and white blood cells, known as cystic acne, which can leave permanent scars. So we need to sort this out quickly as your problem is moving in that direction.'

He had gone very pale. What he was suffering from was every teenager's nightmare. The embarrassment of it would be unbearable.

'I'm going to put you on an antibiotic capsule that is very good for this sort of skin infection. It should attack the bacteria, reduce the inflammation, and prevent it from progressing into what I've just described.'

He was smiling for the first time. 'That's great! You've no idea how much it's been affecting me.'

'Yes, well, you'll have to be patient, you know.' she told him sympathetically. 'The problem isn't going to disappear overnight, but you should soon see an improvement. Come and see me again in a couple of weeks.'

When he'd gone with less of the attitude of the 'leper' in his manner Ruby thought that no matter what age group there was always some health problem that could arise. She knew that only too well from what Robbie had to endure and his was for always, just the same as hers was.

With regard to her first patient of the day his problem should clear up with the right medication and when his body had adjusted to the changes of adolescence.

When the doctors stopped for a brief coffee break in the middle of the morning Libby appeared to say that it was the antenatal clinic in the afternoon that she was usually in charge of, but not today as she had an appointment of that nature herself at the hospital on the lakeside. So Hugo would be taking it instead and she, Ruby, along with one of the practice nurses, would be assisting him.

'Have you done anything like that before?' she asked with a smile for the young doctor who was now part of the practice.

'I haven't done antenatal as such,' Ruby said slowly at the thought of being enclosed with Hugo for a full afternoon, 'but I spent a month on a maternity ward during my hospital training.'

'And how did you find that? Was it enjoyable?' Libby asked.

'Yes and no,' was the reply. 'The feeling of responsibility in helping to bring a new life into the world was awesome and sometimes quite terrifying if complications were present.'

Surprised at the intensity of feeling in her voice Libby said, 'There shouldn't be anything like that today, Ruby. It will be mainly straightforward check-ups on our mothers-to-be and if Hugo finds anything that he *is* concerned about it will be straight to hospital for the patient.'

'Dr Lawrence was very kind when I arrived so unexpectedly,' she said as Libby was about to go back to her own room, 'but once I'd recovered from the traumas of Saturday I did feel that I had spoilt his weekend as he seems to be a very private person.'

'Hugo gave up a position in general practice down south to move to Swallowbrook when his sister's husband died suddenly and she was in a dreadful state, unable to look after herself or her two children properly. He's just come to the end of a gruelling eighteen months that seemed as if it might go on for ever, until Patrice met an old friend over from Canada who persuaded her to go and live there, leaving him free at last to get his own life back.

'When you approached him on Saturday he had just got back from Somerset where he'd been tying up all the loose ends from when he'd lived there, and was probably looking forward to flaking out when he got back, don't you think?' she said laughingly as she observed Ruby's expression.

'Oh, no!' she groaned. 'What a pain he must have thought I was.'

'Hugo can't have thought you too much of a pain if he's offered you the apartment to rent,' Libby said consolingly. 'Nathan and I were amazed because he'd intended leaving it empty as much as possible to avoid noise and interference.'

'He must have seen how much I liked it and taken pity on me,' she said with the gloom of not knowing his circumstances and being too quick to judge heavy upon her.

Whatever the reason there was no time for further discussion. Coffee break was over, it was back to the demands of the day and in what seemed like no time at all it was early afternoon.

The practice nurses were setting out their room to accommodate mothers-in-waiting in the various stages of their pregnancies and Ruby thought that she'd been crazy to think she could avoid Hugo Lawrence while on practice premises, but would try her best to do so when she wasn't...*once the ordeal of tonight's party was over.*

Hugo was impressed by Ruby's efficiency. So far she hadn't exactly filled him with confidence outside the surgery, but there was no fault to be found with the way she was dealing with the pregnant women who had come to be examined.

The practice nurse was taking blood-pressure readings and checking urine samples, while he and Ruby saw each woman in turn to check for problems that could be a cause for alarm with regard to the health of mother and baby.

In one case a patient who was eight months pregnant had been for a hospital check-up the week before and been told that the baby had turned and was in a breech position, and that if it hadn't moved back to where it should be in a fortnight's time they might have to perform a C-section.

She was overwrought and tearful about what was happening, and while Hugo examined her, with Ruby watching intently, she held the distressed woman's hand and stroked her brow.

When he'd finished feeling her swollen stomach gently Hugo told her, 'Your next visit to the hospital will confirm whether the baby is still in the breech position, but they do have the tendency to return to their original position during the last few weeks, and if that doesn't happen you will have all the professional help that is available for a safe birth.'

He had stood by and watched while Ruby dealt with a couple of patients on her own and she'd been conscious of his keen gaze all the while, unaware that his scrutiny was also taking in the pallor of her face and the taut lines of her throat that indicated tension, but only she knew the reason for that and it was how she intended it to stay.

'Well done,' he said when the clinic was over. 'I can see you being ready to do this on your own soon. When Libby finishes you'll be the only woman doctor in the practice and our pregnant patients do prefer a female doctor to be in charge of the antenatal clinic if possible.'

She didn't reply to that, just smiled a pale smile as if the prospect wasn't all *that* exciting, and he thought that maybe she'd been conscious of his doubts about her and now that praise was forthcoming she wasn't going to go overboard with delight.

Instead she said, 'About tonight at Libby and Nathan's place, do I dress up or down? I've only one dress suitable for evening wear.'

Was she kidding? The Gallaghers' supper parties weren't those kinds of occasions. It would be a nice meal, a few drinks, with young Toby sleeping peacefully upstairs and the adults chatting comfortably down below.

'Just casual wear will be fine, I would imagine,' he

told her. 'It will be the kind of thing that the four of us
do at the cottage every couple of months or so and now
that you've joined us it will be five. Do you want a lift?'

The words were out before he'd had time to think
and were at odds with his decision to keep contact out
of working hours to the minimum, but he wasn't to
know that Ruby had been having similar thoughts and
she said airily, 'No, thanks just the same. I'll see you
there, Dr Lawrence.'

'The name is Hugo out of surgery hours,' he told
her, 'just as it will be Libby and Nathan tonight, but I
think that John Gallagher might prefer to be given his
full title. How long is it since you last saw him?'

'Over twelve years. I was fourteen when we moved
to Tyneside because of my father's job and it took me
a long time to get used to it. *It took me a long time to
get used to a few things, but in the end I did,*' she said
flatly, and he wondered what she meant by that.

The two cottages across from the surgery where Libby
and Nathan had lived separate lives until the love they
had for each other had brought them together had just
been made into one as their weekday home. On an island in the middle of the lake was Greystone House
that Nathan had bought Libby as a wedding present
and where they spent their weekends.

As she walked the last few yards to where the lights
of the combined cottages were shining out into the
darkness of a winter evening, Hugo caught her up and
Ruby realised that he must have been a few steps behind as she'd walked the short distance from Lakes

Rise. Surely he wasn't still keeping her under surveillance, she thought as they exchanged polite greetings?

He'd got it wrong again, he was deciding. Ruby must think him insane if he couldn't let her walk a couple of hundred yards without appearing on the scene. She'd be accusing him of stalking next and that would knock him off his pedestal as the most eligible unattached male in the village.

She'd pressed the bell and when the door opened Libby was there with Toby beside her, clean and rosy cheeked in his pyjamas. When he saw Hugo he ran into his arms and he swung him up and held him close.

As Libby watched them fondly the five-year-old cried, 'Can Dr Hugo read me my bedtime story, Mummy Libby?'

'Yes, of course,' she said gently, and as Hugo started to mount the stairs with Toby still in his arms she said to Ruby, 'It is always like this when Hugo comes for supper. He takes Toby up to bed, but first they have a little play and then he reads him a story before he settles down for the night. He is so good with children, was so kind and protective towards those two little nieces of his before Patrice took them to live in Canada.

'Nathan and I are hoping that now the burden has been lifted he might look around the village and find himself a nice wife who will give him some children of his own.'

'Mmm,' Ruby murmured, stuck for words. Personally she couldn't imagine her hermit-like landlord wanting to strike up any sort of romantic union, though he was certainly good looking enough to attract a mate. Yet he did go to The Mallard in the evenings and those kinds of places were renowned for meeting people of the opposite sex.

As Hugo and Toby disappeared on the landing Libby ushered Ruby into a comfortable chintzy sitting room and in a matter of seconds Nathan appeared wearing a striped apron and announced that it was his turn for kitchen duty and could he get her a drink?

'Dad has just rung to say he is on his way,' he told her, 'and is looking forward to seeing you, Ruby, after such a long time.'

Nathan hadn't so far commented on her having lived in Swallowbrook before, or her family being registered with the practice at that time, so she wasn't sure whether he was being tactful, protecting patient confidentiality, or had completely forgotten the trauma that had been present in their lives then and still was for that matter.

Maybe the surgery here had never seen the results that had been in the pipeline as they had been leaving the area and had never known that Robbie's first ever bleed *had* been diagnosed as haemophilia. Hopefully that was how it would be, which would prevent any curiosity regarding herself.

When the elderly retired head of the practice arrived Ruby thought how little he had changed, just a head of silver hair and a few extra lines around kindly blue eyes were the only differences that she could see as they shook hands, and there was nothing to indicate in his manner or words of welcome that he had any particular memories of the time her family had spent in Swallowbrook.

But his many years in general practice had taught John Gallagher caution in his dealings with people. He hadn't forgotten what had happened to the Hollister family, but the young doctor who was observing him anxiously with beautiful brown eyes could rely entirely on his discretion.

With regard to Nathan he hadn't been involved with the family as much as he had, so doubted that any rec-ollections of the child's illness would surface where he was concerned.

That Ruby Hollister had wanted to come back to Swallowbrook was delightful, *and surprising* consid-ering her degree results, so even if her time with them turned out to be short it was most welcome.

Hugo appeared at that moment with the news that Toby was asleep and Ruby observed him curiously. It was as if he was a different person from her rather dour landlord. He was smiling and relaxed, laughing as the others teased him about his friendship with Toby.

'Hugo is like this with all the young ones who come to the surgery,' Nathan said quizzically. 'All the moth-ers ask to see Dr Lawrence when the children aren't well.'

They were taking their seats around the supper table and when Ruby had settled into hers she looked up to find Hugo sitting opposite. Their gazes met and she felt her blood warm. He was a confusing mixture of many things but one of them was clear and unmistakeable— he was the most incredibly attractive man she'd ever met.

Yet from what Libby had said about finding himself

a wife it would seem that he wasn't in any kind of a relationship. Could the reason for that be because until recently every spare moment of his time had been taken up by others?

When the party was over he didn't suggest walking her home. As far as he was concerned, it went without saying that he was going to. It was late, and even walking such a short distance on her own was not acceptable so when he fell in step beside her Ruby didn't argue.

Instead she took him by surprise. 'Why don't we have a stroll by the lake?' she suggested, and glanced up at a full moon in the sky. 'I'd like to see it in moonlight.'

'Yes, if that is what you want,' he said with a shrug of the shoulders. 'But don't forget we both have a date with the practice in the morning, so it hadn't better be for too long, and there *is* a distinct nip in the air.'

'All right,' she told him. 'If you would rather go home I'll take a short walk along the lakeside myself.' And before he could argue she was off, calling over her shoulder, 'I'll see you in the morning, Dr Lawrence, and I promise I won't be late.'

She knew she was behaving stupidly, but she'd felt it again, the lack of desire for her company. He'd been the life and soul of the party in the presence of his friends, but left alone with her he was back to keeping her at a distance whenever possible, except for at the practice when she saw yet another side of him.

If she was expecting him to come after her she was mistaken. Hugo was already striding back up the slope to Lakes Rise and now she was amongst huge trees standing out eerily against the moonlit sky and creatures of the night were scuttling around her feet.

This wasn't what she'd envisaged when she'd suggested that the two of them walk by the lakeside, she thought miserably as tears pricked.

He was the first man she'd ever met who had gripped her imagination to such an extent and her suggestion that they walk by the lake had been born from a longing to be with him for just a little longer before they separated.

The determination to treat him the way he treated her by staying aloof had disappeared during the party and in its place had come a longing to see more of him than less. But his reluctance to be with her any longer than necessary had made her behave stupidly and instead of retracing her steps she lowered herself onto a big boulder at the side of the path and shed a few tears.

The sound of a twig crackling nearby made her dry her eyes and look around her warily and Hugo was there, peering at her and exclaiming, 'Are you insane? Sitting out here in the dark just to prove a point! I haven't been designated as your minder by the surgery or anything like that, yet the role seems to have fallen upon me.'

He took her arm and gently raised her to her feet and at that moment the moon's light was on her face and he saw the tears. 'Ugh!' he groaned. 'You've been crying, Ruby. Why? Whatever for? Didn't you enjoy the party?'

'Yes, it was lovely,' she said between sniffles. 'I've been crying because I'm happier now than I've been in ages.' She was, but the tears hadn't flowed because of that. They had come from a deep hurt inside her that wasn't ever going to go away.

'Does it really mean so much to you, coming back to where you lived when you were young?'

She nodded mutely. It did, it meant a lot, but meeting him meant more, and after what she'd seen and heard tonight she couldn't let it be like that, she just couldn't.

CHAPTER FOUR

THERE was silence between them as each with their own thoughts they walked back to the house overlooking the lake.

Something had happened during the evening to upset Ruby, Hugo decided. They hadn't been tears of happiness that had reddened her eyes and made the smooth pale skin of her face blotchy, but what could it be?

It had been a light-hearted gathering, everyone had made her most welcome, and surely it wasn't his lukewarm reaction to her suggestion that they take a stroll round the lake that had upset her?

It hadn't really been because they had work tomorrow, or that it was chilly in the night air. It was because he had only just got his life back since Patrice had begun to sort hers out, and didn't want any more strings attached at the present time. Though obviously he wasn't going to say that to Ruby, so he'd come up with what had been weak excuses to avoid doing what she'd suggested.

Yet he knew he wasn't helping matters by fussing around her all the time when she was proving to be extremely capable in most things. That was why the tears had been so unexpected.

For her part Ruby was remembering how wonderful he'd been with Toby. Hugo would make a wonderful father for children of his own one day, he was a natural, which was a good enough reason for her to cool it where he was concerned, as when it came to 'mothers' there wouldn't be many less 'natural' than she was.

Yet did she need to proceed carefully with regard to that? It was as if he felt that she was someone to be with as little as possible, and that was one of the reasons why she'd wept, knowing she'd been crazy to suggest they should walk by the lake in the moonlight when he was so obviously keen to get back to Lakes Rise and his new-found peace of mind. If Hugo discovered she was attracted to him, as he would if she didn't conceal it, he really would want to stay clear of her in all but their time at the surgery.

They were at the house. He waited until she'd unlocked the door of the apartment and was about to enter and said, 'Promise me there will be no more tears, Ruby.' She nodded mutely. 'Perhaps some time you'll tell me the real reason why you were so upset.'

'Maybe,' she said in a low voice, knowing that wasn't going to happen. Her nearest and dearest were the only ones who knew the answer to that.

'It surely can't have been because I was reluctant to walk beside the lake,' he persisted.

There was no reply to that, so she just wished him a brief goodnight and went inside, but not to sleep. The thought uppermost in her mind as she lay gazing up at the ceiling was that she'd come to Swallowbrook to realise a dream and it had come true, but what she hadn't come prepared for was that a man like Hugo Lawrence would be featuring largely in her new life.

She'd had dates with some of the guys at medical college, but they'd all been light-hearted affairs without any commitments, none of them had made her blood warm, or caused her to take a good look at what a quirk of nature had done to her, except one.

Having been out with Darren Fielding a few times she'd sensed that he had been getting serious and as she'd liked him well enough had decided that he needed to know about her problem before their relationship progressed any further.

What she'd felt was going to be a difficult moment had been made easier when they'd attended a lecture where amongst various subjects discussed had been haemophilia, with its disastrous effects on both sexes when the illness was present.

When the two of them had gone for a coffee afterwards she'd told Darren that Robbie, her young brother, was a haemophiliac. He'd observed her thoughtfully and then as quick as a flash had wanted to know, 'And where do you fit in with that, Ruby?'

'Having just been to the lecture, where do you think?' she'd said woodenly. 'I'm a carrier of it,' and had watched him swallow hard as his glance had slid away from hers.

In the days that had followed she'd got the message. There had been no more dates or sitting together at lectures. He had avoided her big time and it had made living with the knowledge of what nature had burdened her with harder to cope with than it had been already as she'd realised that bringing her problem out into the open in front of a man who cared for her could result in him running a mile to escape a situation that he hadn't bargained for.

Now she'd met Hugo, a man who under any other circumstances she might have been attracted to, but she was too afraid to enter into any serious relationship. The thought of being rejected again too much to bear.

Common sense said that she should put her Swallowbrook dream to one side and go home, look for a position there away from the effect that he was having on her, but she couldn't bear to do that. It was here that she belonged, working in the practice with the lake and the fells close by.

She was making a big thing out of nothing, she decided as dawn began to lighten the sky. It wasn't as if Hugo was attracted to *her* in any sense of the word. They'd only known each other a short time and for most of it he had been on his guard.

If and when he found himself a 'nice' wife, as Libby and Nathan were hoping he might, it went without saying that it wouldn't be a penniless junior doctor with very average attractions and a tight band of hurt around her heart that wasn't ever going to go away.

Determined to take back control of her life and focus on the reality of why she'd come back to Swallowbrook, the very next morning Ruby phoned the garage where her car was being repaired and was told they were waiting for parts, that it could be another couple of weeks before it was ready for her to collect.

So far she hadn't been out on any home visits from the surgery, but would be doing so soon and the small cream car standing idle on the forecourt was going to have to be used for that purpose.

As she walked towards the practice there was a spring in her step in spite of a sleepless night, as she focussed on her new resolve.

Daffodils were nodding on grass verges at the side of the road, the heavy scent of hyacinths was in the air, and the lake glinting in the rays of a pale sun was once again the same safe place that it had always been in her life. Forgotten were the dark outlines of towering trees etched against a moonlit sky, gone would be the night creatures scuttling to and fro.

Hugo's car was already parked on the forecourt. He must have been up bright and early. There was half an hour to go before the surgery swung into action. Obviously the episode of the night before hadn't kept *him* awake.

At that moment he came out of the surgery building and dangled car keys in front of her. 'For you to borrow,' he informed her. 'We thought you could tag along behind me when I go on house calls today. It will be an advantage, you knowing the area from when you lived here before, Ruby, so maybe you could join me for the first few calls and then strike out on your own with the rest. Would you be happy with that arrangement?'

'Er, yes, I suppose so' she agreed hesitantly. 'I've been looking forward to going out in the district. I checked on my car before I came out and it isn't going to be ready for at least a fortnight.'

He nodded. 'So don't concern yourself. The car is there for your use until your own is.' He wanted to ask if she was all right after the upset of the night before but didn't want to cast any gloom around as she looked happy enough at the moment.

When he left her clutching the car keys and went back inside she looked down at them sombrely. Hugo was still playing safe, she thought. He had managed to avoid having her in the enclosed intimacy of his car.

She wasn't to know that it had been Nathan's idea that they use the two cars for the house calls, and that Hugo had been hoping to have her with him on the chance that she might throw some light on the unexpected upset of the night before. Still, he hadn't pursued the idea because he didn't want the other two doctors to jump to any wrong conclusions. He liked Ruby, admired her keenness and efficiency workwise and her attitude to life in general.

His carefree bachelor days spent down south had included dates with attractive women. There had been dining out, visits to the theatre, and lots of sport in the evenings and at weekends, but when Patrice and her children had needed him so badly he had left it all behind without a moment's hesitation.

Still revelling in his sudden freedom, he hadn't yet had time to hit the high spots again. Just to have his life to himself once more had been enough. The socialising part of it would come later, *but then along had come Ruby in the red cape and part of him hadn't wanted to know, had kept wishing her somewhere else, even though the rest of him wasn't so sure.*

He'd been used to a more mature kind of elegance in his women friends before he'd come to Swallowbrook, but had never met anyone he was interested in enough to want to settle down with, although had always felt that when he did, his choice would be someone like that, and nothing had changed. So why was the girl who was renting his apartment so much in his thoughts?

She was like a breath of fresh air in his life in one way, and an unwelcome intrusion in another, which had been evident the night before when he hadn't agreed to her suggestion that they walk by the lake.

Ruby had been taken aback by it, but she wasn't to know that at the time she'd arrived on the scene he'd been looking forward to spending his time how it suited *him*, doing what *he* wanted for a change.

Maybe if he could find the opportunity to tell her that, she might be less offended by his attitude in general?

They'd done the first two calls together and she'd watched and listened carefully as Hugo had dealt with the third one, a callout to an elderly woman with heart problems who had been very short of breath when they arrived, and living alone hadn't had the strength to call an ambulance as her condition had worsened since she'd asked for a visit from the surgery earlier.

'It is fortunate that we didn't call on Miss Mortimer any later,' Hugo said in a low voice when he'd listened to her heartbeat and felt her pulse. 'Check them for yourself, Dr Hollister, while I request an ambulance urgently.'

When Ruby had done what he'd told her to do she understood the urgency. The other two calls they'd done together had been run of the mill, nothing serious, but not Miss Mortimer's!

After their patient had been taken to hospital and they'd done as she'd requested, locked up everywhere and deposited the key with a neighbour, it was time for Ruby to do the rest of the calls on her own and she suddenly wasn't feeling too confident—would she have reacted as swiftly as Hugo had if faced with Miss Mortimer alone?

'I know that you're not keen on having me around, Dr Lawrence,' she told him, 'that you see me as an encumbrance, but I can't help feeling that this is taking your lack of desire for my company too far.

'Supposing I haven't got the knowledge or experience to deal with any of the calls when on my own, what does it make me look like, and how does it reflect on the practice? Obviously I am going to carry out your instructions but please don't blame me if a patient suffers because I'm new on the job.'

There was a glint of amusement in his glance as he said, 'They are not my instructions, Doctor. Both Libby and I thought it was too soon for you to do home visits on your own, but Nathan, who has a more rugged approach than she and I, suggested it with the thought in mind that it would be good experience, but I prefer to have you with me in my car, so that we can discuss the calls when we've done them. That way you will increase the knowledge and the experience that you're going to need.'

She couldn't resist asking, 'So it wasn't that you didn't want me too much in your face again?'

'Not in this instance, and as for any other occasion when my behaviour was obnoxious I have just one excuse, Ruby. I had just spent a gruelling eighteen months looking after my sister and her family who I love dearly, and the night you arrived I was about to celebrate my freedom.'

'Yes, I know. Libby told me,' she said uncomfortably, 'and then I butted in, all droopy and intrusive. But not having been around at the time you were caring for your family members, and never having had to cope with that sort of situation, I suppose I didn't get the full picture. I am so sorry to have been such a nuisance, Hugo.'

He was smiling. 'Like you've just said, you weren't to know, were you?'

'Maybe not, but the word gatecrasher springs to mind.'

'So does the description selfish blighter, so am I forgiven, Ruby?'

'There is nothing to forgive.' Now it was her turn to smile.

'I'm not so sure about that. Will you let me make amends for last night by taking you for a walk by the lake this evening? And before that why don't I take you for a meal straight from the surgery? There are usually a couple of restaurants open even at this time of the year, so it will save us both the trouble of cooking if we eat out.'

She was observing him wide eyed and he asked whimsically, 'Are you thinking that I'm overdoing the apology?'

Now she was laughing, eyes sparkling, and he thought she was lovely when she was happy.

'No, not at all.' was the reply. 'I can't remember the last time I had two invitations out in a week, or even one for that matter—the supper party last night and dining with you tonight beside the lake will be perfect, I was too young for anything like that when I was here before, so thank you for suggesting it, Hugo.'

He didn't reply to that, just continued to smile and said; 'So as soon as we've finished for the day we'll go and find somewhere to eat.'

'Yes,' she breathed, and as was her custom when happy or excited she felt like doing a little dance of delight, but it could easily be misconstrued, she decided, and didn't want to nip in the bud the new understanding between them by being too presumptuous.

Hugo was checking the time and said, 'So with regard to how you feel about doing the house calls on your own today, we'll park your car here, do them together with you in charge and myself as bystander in case you do come up against something you haven't seen or dealt with before, and we'll collect the car on the way back.'

'Yes, that would be great as long as Dr Gallagher won't be annoyed that I haven't carried out his instructions.'

'No chance,' he assured her. 'Nathan isn't like that.

He is highly delighted with you so far and will always listen to reason. It was a bit too much to ask of you on your first time into house calls, it can be like walking into a minefield sometimes.'

They were back and having a late lunch break before the afternoon surgery when Hugo said, 'You did well, Ruby. Out of a dozen house calls there was really only the one that had you puzzled, but there could have been others. It's all the luck of the draw when out on the district. Nathan understood perfectly when I told him how you'd felt about being left on your own, so we are going to do them as a twosome for the rest of the week.'

He watched her expression lighten and hoped she understood that the togetherness that was suddenly materialising had no motive behind it, other than it was what he would do for any young doctor joining the practice, though he doubted whether asking her out to dine would have been on his agenda if they hadn't had such a downbeat introduction in the first place.

'And with regard to tonight,' he said, 'I rang the hotel on the lakeside as soon as we got back to reserve a table for this evening. That place is always open and the food is good. In a few weeks' time everywhere will be throbbing with life, the shops, the cafés, on the lake, but tonight it should be reasonably quiet.'

It would take the edge off the invitation if there was going to be no time to dress up for it and add some glamour to the occasion, thought Ruby, but at least she wouldn't be dying of hunger while they walked by the lake if they ate first.

As if to emphasise the ordinariness of the occasion he reverted back to surgery talk and said, 'I came across something strange when I was called out to a patient the other day and thought you might be interested to hear about it over dinner.'

'Yes, of course,' she said, and thought that short of putting it in writing that it was going to be just food at the end of a busy day at the practice, Hugo couldn't make it any plainer that he was merely doing the niceties for a newcomer, and wasn't that what she should want it to be for the sake of her peace of mind?

She kept telling herself to put a stop to the attraction she had for him, to control the feelings that he aroused in her, that they had come too fast, too soon. It was only a meal they would be sharing, not a night of passion, and whether he had been tied down with family commitments for quite some time or not, Hugo was too much every woman's dream sort of guy for there not to be someone in his life who would leave a hopeful like herself way behind in the alluring and desirable stakes.

The food *was* good, exceptionally so, and after a long and busy day at the practice the two doctors had concentrated on eating rather than chatting, but now they were having coffee in the hotel lounge and instead of talking shop the first thing Hugo said as they settled into its elegant warmth was, 'So tell me about your family, Ruby. I haven't heard you mention much about them so far. Where is it that they live again?'

'Tyneside,' she replied, immediately wary. 'It's a

lovely part of the country, but it isn't Swallowbrook. I cried buckets when we left here.'

He nodded understandingly. 'Youngsters don't always take well to being uprooted, especially in their teenage years when it means leaving friends behind and having to change schools.'

It was more than that, she thought, much more. Anguish that she couldn't bear to talk about had shattered their lives, most of all Robbie's, and what had happened to him had brought each of them their own pain to cope with as well.

Afraid to give too much away and mindful of her intentions to keep Hugo at arm's length, she sorted through her thoughts, desperate to change the subject. 'You were going to tell me about something unusual that you came across regarding a patient.'

'Ah, yes.' It was registering that Ruby wasn't keen to discuss her private life, which was fine by him. He'd only asked about her family out of politeness.

She wanted to talk shop and he couldn't fault her for that, but felt vaguely irritated for some reason. Yet he was the one who had made it clear that they were just out for a meal and nothing else.

'Muriel Mason is a fifty-year-old ex-teacher who had to take early retirement due to chronic bronchitis,' he told her. 'She'd called me out because her breathing and the cough that is always there were causing her much distress.

'She has a dog, a boxer called Castro. I think in the days when her health was less of a problem she must have been to Cuba.'

Ruby was laughing with head thrown back and even white teeth on view behind lips that he had a sudden urge to kiss, or at the least touch with gentle fingers, and he couldn't believe that he was having those sorts of feelings about someone that he'd known for such a short time.

While he'd lived down south he'd had time to live it up whenever he'd felt like it and was always drawn to curvy blondes with blue eyes, so why on earth was he feeling like this about a girl who was slender, thin almost, with brown eyes and a mane of chestnut hair that would look good in a classy short cut?

He didn't know if she was seeing something in his expression that was putting her on her guard or what, but her amusement was dwindling and she was waiting for what he had to say next about the patient and her dog, so he continued, 'Castro is normally a frisky animal, jumping up at me when I call, but not this time. The poor thing was lying on a blanket on the sofa looking weak and woebegone. When I asked Muriel what was the matter with him she told me to my amazement that he's got Cushing's syndrome. Have you come across the illness at all, Ruby? It's pretty rare.'

She thought for a moment and then said, 'I haven't seen anyone with it, but isn't it connected with adrenaline and the pituitary gland in some way? A disorder caused by abnormally high levels of corticosteroid hormones in the bloodstream? In humans it causes obesity and a humped back?'

'A perfect description of the disease!' he exclaimed. 'It's easy to see why you got a first for your degree. You seem to have life well and truly sorted, with a glowing future in medicine.'

As if, she thought sombrely. There were more important things than being good at the job or the ability to absorb knowledge, such as the contentment that comes with happiness and good health. But at least she'd chosen a profession that cared for mind and body.

Her thoughts went out to Robbie with the blight of haemophilia to cope with all through his life and she was grateful that modern medicine in the form of a concentrate of the V111 factor, the blood-clotting agent, was available to him and others like him when tests showed that the body was running low on its own production of it and could be at risk of a bleed.

She loved her little brother dearly, and always felt that her own problems were minor compared to his, but often in the dark hours of the night they came crowding back and she wept for what she had been denied.

Hugo was observing the changing expressions on her face and they weren't exactly as happy as he'd thought they might have been at the praise he had justly bestowed upon her.

The coffee cups were empty and the moon was there again, lighting up the sky. If they were going to stroll by the lake now was the time, and then for what was left of the evening he was going to see Ruby safely inside the apartment and in the quiet of Lakes Rise get up to date with recent medical journals that had been delivered to the surgery.

That was the plan and it was working as they stood at the water's edge and gazed out across the moonlit water to where Libby and Nathan's second home stood in tranquil solitude on the island in the middle of the lake.

The two of them were so fortunate, thought Ruby, madly in love, spending their working lives in the medical practice of this beautiful place and raising their adopted son. Soon they would reach the height of their happiness when their baby was born.

The feeling of melancholy that had been there when they had been having coffee was back, not because she envied them their lovely life but because hers was always going to be a matter of 'if only'.

Hugo was standing just behind her when, haunted by her thoughts, she felt that if she stayed a moment longer, absorbing the beauty of the moon's light on the water and the fells ruggedly silhouetted against a silver sky, she would want to weep.

She turned swiftly, cannoned into him and would have overbalanced if he hadn't been there with arms reaching out to steady her... And then they were around her...he was holding her close and she was liking it, liking it a lot. When she looked up into his face Hugo was smiling, but there was a question in his gaze. 'So why the sudden rush to get away from here?'

'There isn't any,' she said softly from inside the magic circle of his hold. 'I just had a funny moment but you've made it go away.' And though her voice wasn't asking him to kiss her, it was there in her eyes.

Unable to resist the appeal of her, he bent and brushed his lips against hers, then put her away from him gently and said, 'I think we should make tracks,

Ruby. It's late and I have things to do when I get in, as I'm sure you have too.'

She nodded. They'd stepped from behind the border-lines of their acquaintance for a few magical moments and now Hugo was ready to call halt.

They walked back to the car more quickly than when they'd strolled away from it earlier and within minutes he pulled up on the drive of Lakes Rise, and as she was reaching for the doorhandle, he said, 'See you tomorrow, Ruby. Bye for now.'

'Thanks for the meal, Hugo,' she said, not willing to be dismissed so quickly. 'It was the nicest food I've had in ages. It has been a lovely evening. I didn't want it to end.'

'But it had to, didn't it?' he said gravely.

'Not for me,' she said in a low voice, and then she was out of the car and walking quickly towards the apartment and he made no attempt to follow her.

Once inside Ruby stood gazing blindly into space. This thing she felt for Hugo was what she had always tried to avoid, especially after Darren's brush-off. A casual fling, the odd date she could cope with, but this could lead to the kind of heartache that was soul destroying.

Not for him, but for her. Hugo was showing all the signs of caution and didn't even know about the night-mare that she lived with. His butterfly kiss had been an indication of him not wanting to take the moment any further and his speedy dismissal the moment they were back had been another clear indication that he was in no mood to dawdle.

She was getting the message from two directions—her own common sense, which had been in short supply ever since their moment of meeting, and his reluctance to get too close to her. From now on she was not going to let the attractions of her landlord get to her in any shape or form.

Tomorrow was Friday, the last day they would be doing the home visits together, and maybe if she told them at the practice that she felt confident enough now to cope on her own they would agree to her going solo on the last day of the week.

With that thought in mind she went to bed filled with determination and purpose and surprisingly slept the moment she laid her head on the pillow.

Not so for Hugo. With the medical journals untouched he sat late into the night, gazing across to where Ruby was deep in dreamless sleep.

They'd met too soon, he thought. No sooner had he got his life back after Patrice and the children had gone than Ruby had arrived on the scene, tired and bedraggled after a stressful day, and she had never been out of his thoughts since.

But of late they were not the same kind of thoughts that he'd had then, when he'd had to involve himself in looking after her wellbeing whether he'd wanted to or not. As he'd watched her dancing around the apartment on the night she'd become his tenant, as well as amusement there had been an unexpected feeling of tenderness inside him, and whenever he had cause to congratulate her on her knowledge and expertise in the surgery it was there again, a warm tide of feelings washing over him.

He was trying to stay aloof from the physical appeal she had for him, but the memory of moments like tonight when she'd ended up in his arms for a few mind-blowing seconds and had let him see how much she liked it were not going to go away.

In spite of having made a big thing about tonight's dining out together being just a form of apology for being so boorish when they'd first met if he was honest with himself it had been more than that.

He'd wanted her to himself for a few hours, away from the surgery and Lakes Rise, in neutral surroundings where he could get to know her better, and it had taken some degree of will power to wish Ruby a brief goodnight and point himself towards the house, when only a short time ago he would have been fretting to get back home to his freedom from care.

Maybe he was beginning to feel like this about her because with Ruby he had a choice—she asked nothing of him. With Patrice and her children there had been *no choice* and he had let it cloud his judgement in those first days of Ruby's arrival in the village.

He went up to bed at last with no answers for his thoughts and wondered what tomorrow would have in store for the two of them.

The main topic of conversation at the surgery the next morning was that Gordon, the elderly practice manager, had decided to retire, and the news was generating pleasure because they were all invited to a meal at the end of the month on his last day, and side by side with the pleasure was curiosity as to who would be taking his place.

For Ruby, who had just expressed to the other doctors her confidence regarding going it alone on the home visits and got their approval, the retirement of the practice manager wasn't of that much interest because she hardly knew him, and did she want to socialise in Hugo's company once more and start the heart-searching all over again?

The days were flying by and their relationship in the surgery was good, but almost non-existent away from it.

She had discussed how she was attracted to him at length with her mother and Jess Hollister's heart had twisted to hear that her beloved daughter might have met the man of her dreams and was having to do all she could to put him out of her thoughts, which wasn't going to be easy, working in the same environment.

'Shouldn't you explain the circumstances to him?' she'd suggested gently. 'There might be a way round it.'

'Mum, we both know that there isn't, don't we?' she'd said, 'and in any case the attraction is all on my part. Hugo seems intent on keeping things strictly business, so there really is no need to worry about my feelings for him.'

CHAPTER FIVE

As the night of the practice manager's farewell approached spring was settling upon Swallowbrook in all its fresh delight, with new lambs in the fields of the surrounding farms, green shoots on the branches of the trees, and the fells had lost the gaunt look of winter.

The cafés and shops were filling up with early visitors, the village was alive again, and the magic of it was helping Ruby to count her blessings and be sensible by keeping out of Hugo's way other than at the practice, which wasn't too difficult as he was thinking along similar lines.

Yet it wasn't blotting out his curiosity about her, or slowing down the racing of his pulse when she was near. He knew he could take his pick of several attractive women locally who were free agents if he wanted to, and that to keep Ruby on the fringe of his life was the right thing to do, but neither solution appealed to him because those moments beside the lake when he'd kissed her kept coming back. How her eyes had been wide with wonderment as she'd looked up at him from the circle of his arms, and how he'd managed to control the desire she'd awakened in him and had merely brushed his lips against hers.

The leaving event was to take place at the hotel where Hugo had taken Ruby to eat that night straight from the surgery. It would be the second retirement from the Swallowbrook practice in recent months with John Gallagher having stepped down not long before, and Gordon was planning a big affair.

Although an elderly bachelor, he had many friends and a scattered family who would all be coming for the occasion, as well as all the surgery staff and the local chemist.

The invitations asked that guests and their partners should wear evening dress, reminding Ruby that whilst she had the dress, she'd no one to escort her. The obvious solution was not to go, to send her apologies with some sort of believable excuse, as she wouldn't know anyone if she did go, apart from the folks at the surgery, and they would be with husbands and wives or partners.

She knew that Libby and Nathan were having to take Toby with them for lack of a reliable childminder and suggested that she would look after him if they wished as she was too new to the village as it was now to fit in well with those present at the retirement party, and Hugo, according to surgery gossip, was bringing one of the medical reps who'd been invited.

They were reluctant to accept her offer at first, but she insisted that it would be a pleasure, which was true compared to being the odd one out at the gathering, so it was arranged that she would go to the cottage across from the surgery at seven o'clock on the evening of the event and take care of Toby.

She would enjoy looking after him, she was thinking as she drove down to the cottage on the night of the party, and it would take her mind off Hugo and the medical rep, who was glamorous and glossy and would be a perfect foil for his dark attractiveness.

She was unaware that taking the rep to the party was something that Hugo had been loath to do, but Bryony Matthews had told Libby that she would love to come if she could sit next to him, so he'd reluctantly agreed to do the honours.

Reluctant because he'd been intending asking Ruby if she would be his partner. He had wanted to allow himself the treat of spending the evening with her. Just being with her at the surgery was beginning to feel like not enough. He kept telling himself it was crazy with them living so close, yet seeing so little of each other out of surgery hours.

He was coming to terms with her presence in his life, aware that she was different from other women he'd met, with none of the vanities and ploys that some of her sex had attempted to use to get him into bed... without succeeding. Any moves in that direction would come from him, when if ever he felt that the time was right.

Ruby made him smile, and at the same time made him curious about what was underneath the mixture of competence that she displayed in the surgery and her lack of confidence otherwise. Yet she'd obviously found herself a partner for the night of Gordon's party, as there had been no softening on her part in their unspoken determination to cool it between them and he hadn't felt the need to ask who.

Sufficient that he had been lumbered with Bryony Matthews, who he was far from keen on as she always brought personal matters into the conversation when she called at the surgery to push a new drug that her company was merchandising.

No doubt it would be the same tonight, he thought grimly as he dressed for the evening ahead, but Libby had asked him to partner Bryony as a favour because she belonged to one of the top pharmaceutical firms in the country and always gave Swallowbrook priority regarding what was going on in the world of medication.

Yet there could be one consolation during the evening ahead. If he could get her alone he was going to explain to Ruby what his intention had been before he had been shanghaied into entertaining Bryony.

It was against his nature to allow himself to be put in a situation like the one with the pharmaceutical rep when he was wanting to get to know Ruby better. Apart from the fact that she was the junior doctor at the practice and had once lived in the village, he knew very little about her. She kept information about her family to a minimum as well as everything else she'd been involved in before appearing in his life, yet why shouldn't she keep her affairs to herself if she wanted to? Ruby was doing a good job as one of the doctors of the Swallowbrook Medical Practice, so why couldn't he accept that was all that mattered?

Patrice rang from Canada just as he was about to leave the house and by the time she'd finished chatting he was on the last minute for the party.

The apartment was in darkness so obviously Ruby had already left and there would be no time to speak to her before the meal, which was before the presentation that the practice was making to Gordon, so it would be halfway through the evening before he got the chance to be near her.

When he entered the dining room of the hotel the first thing he saw was a pouting Bryony patting the seat of the empty chair beside her. As he hurried across to join her his eyes were raking the room to find Ruby and it soon registered that she wasn't there, and neither was the opportunity to find out why as the hotel staff were already coming round with the food.

The meal was over, the presentation had been made, and the guests were mingling by the time he got the chance to ask Libby where Ruby was. He had a ghastly sinking feeling that she was ill, alone in the apartment or something similarly unpleasant, and was dumbstruck when she said, 'Ruby had no one to come with, Hugo, and so offered to babysit for us to save us having to bring Toby to something that is far past his bedtime.'

'Oh, I see!' he exclaimed. 'Why didn't she tell me she had no one to partner her?'

'She would have known you were going to be with Bryony, wouldn't she? So obviously she wouldn't push

herself forward,' she said mildly, surprised by his reaction.

'Yes, I suppose so,' he agreed begrudgingly.

'If you want to speak to her we'll be going in about
an hour and then she'll be free,' she informed him, 'but
don't expect her to come here, Hugo, she isn't dressed
for it.'

'No, of course not,' he replied, and thought there was
nothing to stop him from going there…now!

After noting that Bryony had a circle of male guests
gathered around her he said to Libby, 'I'm going to pop
round to your place if that's all right with you.'

When she nodded, still bemused, he went striding
off, the most attractive man in the room, resplendent in
black dinner jacket and trousers, dazzling white shirt
and bow-tie, not caring a damn how he looked or that
Bryony's gaze was following him.

He couldn't bear the thought that Ruby had been
tucked away like some sort of outcast at Libby and
Nathan's cottage while he'd been…what? Not enjoying
himself, that was for sure, because the moment he'd realised she wasn't at the party it had died a death, and
now he was going to go and find out why she hadn't
told him what she was planning to do.

Having been bathed, fed and read to, Toby had fallen
asleep on the sofa and Libby had just picked him up
gently and was about to carry him up to bed when the
bell rang.

With Toby cradled against her, she went to the door
and, managing to lift the latch with some degree of dif-

ficulty, found Hugo in the porch, and the sight of him took her breath away.

'Can I come in?' he asked.

'Er…yes.' she said, unable to conceal her amazement. 'But keep your voice down. If Toby awakens at the sound of it he could take forever to go back to sleep.' Her voice had trailed away as he'd stepped inside in all his magnificence, and finding it again she said, 'I was just taking him up to bed.'

'So it would seem. Give him to me,' he told her, with his annoyance abating and tenderness taking its place at the sight of her with the sleeping child in her arms. As she obeyed and followed him up the stairs she couldn't believe that her Cinderella position had been reversed. Prince 'not so' Charming, if his expression was anything to go by, had arrived.

As Hugo watched her gently tucking Toby beneath the covers he said, 'He's a great little guy. I wouldn't mind a house full of children like him one day.'

When she straightened up there was yearning in her expression, or maybe something deeper, he thought. Did it border on sadness? Yet she was smiling as they went down the stairs together and at the bottom she turned to him and asked, 'So how can I help you, Hugo?' and the spell of the moments of togetherness they'd just shared was broken.

'I'm here because you've missed Gordon's party, for one thing,' he said flatly, 'and for another because you didn't tell me you intended giving it a miss because you had no one to go with. Why didn't you let me know what you had in mind?'

'You're asking why!' she exclaimed. 'Why do you think? We haven't exactly been communicating of late out of working hours, have we? And you were hooked up for the evening with the pharmaceuticals rep. I didn't think you would want a threesome.'

'Quite right, I wouldn't have, but it would have been Bryony who was the surplus one. I was furious when Libby told me you were here looking after Toby while the rest of us were being wined and dined.'

He wasn't going to explain that he'd looked for her in vain amongst the guests and been dismayed to discover that she wasn't there, though in truth he had only himself to blame for not checking out her arrangements for the evening beforehand.

'You're making a fuss about nothing, Hugo,' she said calmly, and as he observed her dressed in jeans and a cotton top that contrasted sharply with his own elegance the comment brought his disappointment to a head.

Before she could resist she was in his arms and this time the gentleness of that other occasion was replaced by a need that was raw and demanding as he said softly, 'Fussing, am I? We'll see.'

It was no gentle brushing of his lips against hers this time. He kissed her until she was gasping for breath, weak and pliant in his arms, and it had to stop! As she wrenched herself away from him she said weakly, 'That has just made everything more confusing for both of us.'

What had just happened had left her feeling so vulnerable she could have wept because that was what she couldn't afford to be. She had to make him see that they couldn't be anything more than colleagues and friends.

She didn't want it to be like that, it would be so easy to let the attraction they were developing for each other take its course and fall in love with this wonderful man. But to end it now would be the least painful solution in the long run and in keeping with that line of thought she said, 'Please don't do that again. It was totally un-called for.'

'Maybe, maybe not,' he replied levelly.

Before he had the chance to make any further ambiguous comments she said, 'I think you should go, Hugo. It will seem odd if Libby and Nathan find you here when they come back from the party.'

'Yes, maybe I should,' was his answer to that, 'but I hope you realise that I wouldn't have come here if you hadn't been so cagey about your arrangements. Libby asking me to partner Bryony was a diplomatic move on behalf of the practice that I could hardly have refused to fall in with, or I would have been taking you.'

'You seem to be missing the point,' she told him. 'I didn't mind coming here to look after Toby. I insisted, in fact, so that Libby and Nathan could stay as long as they liked without having to take him with them to something that could be over quite late.'

She wasn't going to explain that she'd decided if she couldn't be with him at the gathering, the next best thing would be to do a favour for the other two doctors by babysitting for them. Better Hugo should think that his place in her world was only on the edges of it.

He was about to do as she'd requested and go back

to the party, having made a fiasco of coming to seek her out. But he'd been driven to do it by the disappointment of finding her not there and had come to discover what her motives had been in offering to stay with Toby when there must have been other members of the village community that Libby and Nathan would have trusted with the task.

But the moment he'd seen her with Toby in her arms and observed how gentle she was with him his thoughts had moved into other channels and he had found himself picturing her with children of her own, patient and caring beneath the mantle of motherhood, the kind of woman he would choose for a wife one day.

Unaware of the direction of his thoughts, she was observing him questioningly and bringing them into line he said, 'I'm going back to the party, Ruby. Sorry to have disturbed you.' And before she had the chance to speak he was in his car with the engine running and within seconds disappeared from sight.

She watched him go dry eyed, but was weeping inside. What had just happened between them had made her even more aware of the futility of her feelings for him. For a few ecstatic moments she'd felt that she was where she belonged, in Hugo's arms, but reality had been sharp in following those sentiments and nothing had changed, she told herself bleakly.

When Libby and Nathan came home not too long afterwards, concerned that they might be keeping her too long in her role as babysitter, she was leafing through a magazine, outwardly tranquil with no indication that not so long ago she had been kissed until she was breathless by the fourth member of the practice.

Yet Libby was observing her thoughtfully, remembering how Hugo had disappeared as soon as she'd told him why Ruby wasn't at the party, how he'd gone looking anything but festive and returned in an even more sombre mood.

She liked Ruby, who was an intelligent and caring addition to the practice but hardly likely to catch Hugo's eye, she would have thought. But he'd been bogged down with his sister's affairs from the moment of arriving in Swallowbrook, hadn't had a moment to call his own, and now it was different, he was living his own life for a change and if Hugo had set his sights on Ruby, good for him.

When Ruby arrived back at the apartment the house beside it was in darkness so Hugo must still be living it up at the party, not intending letting their earlier skirmish spoil his evening, and could she blame him?

He'd come to the cottage out of concern for her and she'd been quite odious, especially after he'd taken her breath away with the kisses that had come out of nowhere, so he'd obviously gone back to where there was warmth, laughter and friendship, and on that assumption she went upstairs to bed but, as was getting to be a habit, it wasn't to sleep.

Hugo was watching the time and wasn't in party mood. The room hired for Gordon's retirement party was gradually emptying as midnight was approaching, but *he* wasn't able to leave yet as, wanting to relieve Ruby of her duties back at the cottage, Libby and Nathan had asked if he would stay until the end and see the elderly practice manager safely home as he was drinking quite a lot of champagne. And then there was Bryony to chauffeur back to her hotel in the town, so it was a cert that Ruby would not be awake when he finally arrived home.

The pharmaceutical rep had enjoyed herself hugely at the party in the company of various unattached men, but had commented on the way home, after they'd seen Gordon safely inside, that she hadn't seen much of him and if she'd known that he was going to be here, there and everywhere during the evening she might have thought twice about putting in an appearance.

But any slight niggles she might have had disappeared when after stopping outside her hotel he produced out of the boot of his car one of the beautiful flower arrangements that had graced the gathering and presented it to her. Once that was accomplished he breathed a sigh of relief and set off for home.

He was wrong in thinking that Ruby would be asleep when he arrived home. She heard his car pull up on the drive and tiptoed to the window without putting on the light. The sight of the tall figure in evening dress walking towards the house made her want to run out to him and explain what it was that had always made her stay clear of serious relationships with men.

Hugo was a doctor, for heaven's sake, and if she couldn't tell him, who could she tell? Yet she couldn't bear the thought of watching the light go out of his eyes with the telling of it, as there was always Darren Fielding's reaction to take into account.

She awoke the next day to the sound of the bells of the old Norman church pealing out over the village on a Sunday morning in spring and saw that the sun was already shining in a cloudless blue sky. With the sound and the sight of those things there came the urge to be beside the lake, away from all unhappy thoughts.

The eating places beside the water would be already open so why not go and have breakfast there and then renew her acquaintance with the nearest of the fells for a while? That way she wouldn't be spending the morning wondering if and when Hugo was going to appear.

When she walked into her favourite place she saw immediately that she didn't have to wait for that to happen. He was already up and about, a solitary diner seated at a table in the corner with his attention centred on the cooked breakfast in front of him, and she almost groaned.

The events of the night before were still painfully clear. She hadn't wanted to meet up with him again so quickly. Tomorrow at the surgery would have been soon enough, but it was as if some unseen force had taken over her life and if she didn't make a quick departure it would be there again, strong and compelling, drawing her to him like a magnet.

As she turned to leave he looked up and, putting down his knife and fork, got to his feet and came across to where she was hovering in the doorway.

'What's the matter, Ruby?' he asked in a low voice. 'I don't bite. Why not join me for breakfast? I can recommend the food. I always come here on Sundays and then go walking on the fells, weather permitting.'

He hadn't slept much after arriving home in the early hours. Had kept remembering how she'd felt so right in his arms and how after the first few seconds she'd succumbed to his passion, but it had all ended on a flat note when she'd asked him not to kiss her again.

Finally after much introspection he'd rejected the idea of having a lie-in and had kept to his usual routine, which would take him out of Ruby's line of vision from the apartment, but it was as if she'd read his mind. She was here in the bistro beside the lake dressed for fell walking, if he wasn't mistaken, in a checked shirt, jeans, a warm jacket, boots and with a woolly hat on her head.

'Yes. I know you don't bite,' she said in a low voice, 'but the other things you do are just as painful.'

She was following him to the table and he said whimsically, 'So I'm not the charmer I thought I was. I can't recall any woman I've kissed before describing it in those terms. Maybe I've been ranking myself too high.'

'Don't make fun of me, Hugo,' she said as she seated herself opposite him. 'I am not "any" woman. I'm my own person and will let you know when I want to be kissed, *if ever.*'

The pleasure of seeing her appear in the doorway of the café was still strong upon him and letting that comment pass he pointed to the menu and said, 'At least let me buy you breakfast,' and beckoned for one of the staff to come to take her order.

The food was good and having finished his own meal Hugo sat back in his chair and watched her enjoy what was put in front of her. At one point he said, 'Do I take it that you are dressed for fell walking?'

She nodded. 'Yes. I am. It's quite some time since my dad used to take me up there. He was a keen walker and loved this place like I do. It was a blow for him when we had to move because of his job.'

Her mobile phone rang at that moment and Hugo saw her stiffen as if it was a rare occurrence and could be a cause for anxiety, but her expression cleared as she listened to what the caller had to say and in reply told them, 'I'll try to collect it today if I can. What time do you close on Sundays? Twelve-thirty? I'll do my best, otherwise it will be next Saturday.'

When she'd switched off Ruby said, 'That was about Theodora. She's ready to be collected.' As he observed her blankly, she added, 'Theodora is my car. A clapped-out old banger compared to the car I've been using since I came here, but dear to my heart nevertheless, and I don't want to have to wait another week before she is returned to me. So I need to get moving if I'm going to be there before the garage closes. Once I've sorted out train times I'll be off. Thanks for inviting me to breakfast, and now I must dash.'

'Hold on,' he said, gently pushing her back down onto her seat.

'Where is this garage?'

'In Manchester, which is quite some distance away.

It was the nearest one when the car came to a stand-still and I asked the breakdown people to take it there. They've been ages sorting out the problem and order-ing spare parts.'

'No need to start chasing off to the nearest station,' he said calmly. 'Trains can be few and far between on Sundays. I'll take you.' Her eyes widened at the offer. 'Maybe you'd better go back to the apartment to change into more suitable shoes first, and me too. We can't drive with heavy boots on our feet.'

As she nodded, still in a state of surprise, he went to pay for their food and once that was done they walked quickly back to the apartment, where she changed her footwear and collected the cash she'd been saving to pay for the repairs. Then they were off, together again whether she wanted them to be or not.

There was silence as his car ate up the first few miles with its powerful engine and Ruby was happy with that. No talking meant no awkward moments, until out of the blue Hugo asked, 'Are you going home for Mothering Sunday in a couple of weeks' time?'

'Yes,' she replied, surprised by the question. 'I would never want to miss *that*.'

There was something in her tone that made him take his glance off the road for a second to observe her ex-pression and he saw sadness in it.

What was it that Ruby was hiding with regard to her background? Whatever it was she wasn't going to be telling the likes of him, that was for sure. She had already made it clear that her private life was a no-go area as far as he was concerned.

After that any conversation between them was just casual stuff regarding the weather and how long he expected them to be before they reached the outskirts of Manchester so that she could be reunited with the treasured Theodora.

They did discuss one serious matter but it was surgery related and of interest to them both—Gordon's replacement as practice manager. He had suggested his niece for the job with the information that she had worked in administration of various sorts and was coming to live in his house once he had taken up residence in a Spanish villa that he'd bought.

'Laura is on her own with two children,' he'd told the three senior doctors, 'and running this place would fit her like a glove.' So on his recommendation they had asked her to come for an interview the following week and Ruby was curious to know what Hugo thought of the idea.

He was smiling. 'It's wait-and-see time, Ruby. Gordon speaks highly of her but he once recommended a cleaner for the surgery and she didn't know a vacuum cleaner from a lawnmower.

'If she gets the job his niece won't be starting for a while. He's moving to Spain in Easter week and Gordon says that she intends having some work done on the house to suit her own tastes, which could be tricky with regard to organising it as she will be moving up here from the Midlands with two children to consider in whatever she plans to do.

'Why can't we talk about you for a change?' he suggested. 'You always clam up for some reason when I try to do that. I get the feeling that you have strong family ties but don't want to talk about them.'

'Yes, I do have a great relationship with my parents and young brother and, no, I don't want to talk about it,' she replied. And when a sign ahead on the motorway indicated Manchester five miles, 'We'll be at the garage in a matter of minutes, Hugo.'

They were, and when she saw Theodora waiting for her Ruby's face lit up. Going to the car, she traced her hands gently along the bonnet and watching her Hugo thought once again how different she was from all other women he had known. It was an old car, a much-out-of-date model with nothing to catch the eye about it, yet to Ruby it was supreme.

CHAPTER SIX

BEFORE they set off on the return journey Hugo said, 'We'll stop off for lunch somewhere, I think, either at one of the motorway services or maybe find a place to eat when we turn off. I'll drive in front and keep a lookout for somewhere while you follow in Theodora, if that's all right with you.'

She nodded, in a state of bliss to have her car back and to be spending the day with Hugo without any strings attached. A sandwich by the roadside and a bottle of water would do fine as far as she was concerned, but she doubted that he had anything so mundane in mind.

They'd just left the motorway and he was ahead of her on a quiet side road when the driver of a car in the process of overtaking her lost control and, missing Theodora by inches, ended up in a ditch by the roadside.

Ruby slammed on the brakes, and flinging herself out of her car ran towards it.

A woman in her thirties or thereabouts was slumped unconscious over the steering-wheel when she looked inside and to her horror there was a baby wailing in distress fastened in a child's seat in the back of the car.

Hugo had appeared beside her, having seen the crashed car so narrowly miss hers from where he'd been driving a short distance in front.

Its doors were locked, as was to be expected, smoke was rising from the engine, there was a strong smell of petrol, and aware of the fire hazard in such circumstances he said, 'Phone the emergency services fast, Ruby,' and called over his shoulder as he ran towards his car, 'I'm going to have to prise the doors open. There's a spade in the boot of my car, maybe the flat edge of that will do it.' The smoke continued to seep out of the bonnet. 'We need to get them both out fast.'

The spade did what was required of it and as the door on the driver's side of what was a small two-door model came open he left Ruby to examine the injured woman as best she could and ran round to the passenger side to give the door there the same treatment, and once again it was successful.

The baby's wailing was now a protesting howl and as Hugo tried to reach it to release the safety straps that were holding it firmly in the car seat it became clear that there wasn't going to be enough room for him to get near enough.

Ruby was bending over the unconscious woman, feeling her pulse with one hand and trying to stop the bleeding from face wounds where she'd hit the windscreen with the other. Aware of the lack of space he was encountering, she straightened up and said, 'I'll get the baby, Hugo.'

If the car went up in flames while she was inside it with the child and he couldn't get them out in time he would want to die too, he thought raggedly, but he nodded grimly and watched as easing herself inside she began to fiddle with the straps that had been out of his reach. Once they'd come loose she reached for the frightened child and eased herself backwards until she was near enough to pass it into his waiting arms, and then they both ran round to the other side to check on the mother.

At that moment they heard the welcome sound of sirens and as she stood looking down at the crying baby in her arms while Hugo prepared to explain the situation to the emergency services, it seemed as if on the surface it was unharmed.

But the staff in A and E would be the best judge of that, and as an ambulance and fire engine arrived simultaneously, a paramedic took the little one gently from her, and while the fire service personnel began the task of getting the mother out of the car with as little further injury as possible, Ruby and Hugo stood by and watched gravely.

The police came next to control the traffic that had been building up since the accident, and in response to their questions Hugo told them, 'We are both doctors from the Swallowbrook Medical Practice and were travelling in separate cars when the baby's mother tried to overtake Dr Hollister and lost control. That is basically all we can tell you, but if you need to speak to us further you can reach us at the practice or on our home phones.'

After watching mother and baby being taken into the ambulance and a breakdown vehicle arrive to remove the damaged car, Hugo said sombrely, 'That was a nightmare, Ruby, that I wouldn't want to experience again. The car could have gone up in flames any moment, yet you were so calm. You continue to amaze me as I get to know you better, and that is what I want, to get to know you better, so please don't keep backing off from me.'

She swallowed hard, praise indeed from the man of her dreams, but he was the man of her nightmares too, the nightmares that she'd had to live with for the last twelve years, and if she gave in to the attraction he had for her and she for him, she would be involving him in them and it just wouldn't be fair to put that burden onto a man who wanted a house full of children like Toby.

When Robbie had been diagnosed a haemophiliac and her mother had been discovered to be the carrier of the defective gene it had changed everything for Ruby too. She was tested and found she too was a carrier and could inflict upon a son of her own the miseries of what Robbie had to endure, or pass on the carrier gene to a daughter along with the dreadful feeling of inadequacy that was always there when she thought about the future.

It hadn't hit her so much at first. In her early teens she'd brushed it to one side, but as she'd grown older the magnitude of the problem had hit her like a sledgehammer. She'd gone for genetic counselling and finally made the heartbreaking decision that she wasn't going to have any children.

She'd been doing well so far with casual dates that meant little to her, but had always known that the day would come when she would meet 'the one'! The man she would love for ever. She'd often wondered how would she cope with that and now the time of testing might be here, unless she could keep Hugo on the fringe of her life.

'Thanks for those kind words, Hugo, and obviously we *are* going to get to know each other better to a degree, both of us working at the practice and you being my landlord, and I will be quite happy with *those* arrangements as they stand.'

He sighed. Ruby couldn't make it much plainer how she felt about their relationship, and not so long ago he would have been happy to hear her comments, but not so much now.

The degree of his disappointment when she hadn't been at Gordon's party the night before had shaken him with the force of it and brought into focus how much it was beginning to mean to him having her near.

When they'd met unexpectedly at the lakeside café early that morning he'd been only too happy to offer to take her to pick up her car. It would give him the opportunity to spend some prime time with her, he'd thought, help to lessen the disappointment of her non-arrival at the party, and that was how it had been, until in the aftermath of the accident she'd made light of his praise and the suggestion that they see more of each other.

'I'm not sure if by what you've just said you are letting me off lightly, or are deliberately misunderstanding me,' he commented flatly, 'so shall we get back into our cars and point ourselves homeward once more?'

'Yes' she agreed meekly, and thought they wouldn't be stopping to eat somewhere after *that* and she was starving, but she was wrong. He pulled up outside a restaurant beside one of the smaller lakes in the area and when she drew level said, 'I suggest that we stop off here.'

She nodded, willing to agree to anything after that childish attempt to warn him off, and as they were shown to a table said in a low voice, 'I think it's time that you were my guest, Hugo.'

'Not at all,' he said dryly. 'It was my idea that we stop here.'

They ate the food put before them in silence and were soon on the last lap of the journey with Swallowbrook not far away, to Ruby's relief.

She was desperate to be back in the apartment with just her own thoughts to answer to, and as soon as they both pulled up on the drive of Lakes Rise she was out of her car and after thanking him for taking her to Manchester and for the meal they'd stopped off for, she was gone.

The simplest thing would be to find a job near home instead of continuing to live her dream in Swallowbrook, she thought once she was inside the apartment and huddled in a chair by the window. That way she would be immune from the longing that Hugo aroused in her and hopefully in time she might forget him.

When she looked up he was striding purposefully

across the short distance that separated the apartment from the house and a moment later was ringing the bell. She opened the door to him reluctantly and as if he had read her mind Hugo said, 'Just a quick word. I've been on to the hospital about the mother and baby and they told me that the reason for her losing control of the car was because she'd had a heart attack, which it was impossible for us to diagnose from the position she was in.'

'And what's the situation now?' she asked anxiously.

'She's in Coronary Care and has fractures of the cheekbones from being slammed against the windscreen, but she'll survive.'

'And the baby?'

'Being kept in for observation, but so far no problems. The husband is with them both and in a state of shock as neither he nor his wife were aware that she had a heart defect.'

He was turning to go and said over his shoulder, 'I'm not expecting *you* to need *me* for anything, but if you do I'll be in The Mallard as the night is still young.' And off he went, the tall raven-haired man with clear blue eyes who had unknowingly turned her life upside down.

With a yearning to hear the voice of someone who understood she rang home and when her father's voice came over the line it was as welcome as her mother's always was, sometimes even more so because Ruby knew that always behind her mother's apparent calm and cheerfulness there was a deep sorrow that came from what nature had done to her.

'And so how's my girl?' he asked.

'Not bad,' she said. 'I just needed to hear a voice I knew. How is Robbie, is he all right? And Mum, how is she?'

'They're both fine,' he told her, knowing how much she needed to hear that. Only he knew about the black pit of depression that her mother had to climb out of sometimes. 'Robbie is at the local youth club and your mother has gone to the cinema with a friend, so no cause for worry there, Ruby. She's looking forward to seeing you on Mother's Day. Have you got the car back yet, or do I need to come and fetch you?'

'Theodora is back where she belongs I'm pleased to say, so no problem regarding transport. I'll drive down on Saturday morning and come back late Sunday night.'

When they'd finished chatting Ruby went back to the window again and gazed out into the night. Her father would have gone back to his favourite chair in front of the television. Her mother was at the cinema, Robbie at the youth club, and with a pull at her heartstrings she knew Hugo was relaxing in The Mallard. He was everything she'd ever wanted, caring and kind, generous in his praise when they'd been involved with the mother and baby in the car crash. He'd even told her that he wanted to get to know her better, which would have been like music to her ears under other circumstances, but little did he know that was the one thing she couldn't promise.

Yet he'd obviously rallied from what she'd said about that because he'd gone to join residents and tourists in the popular Mallard for the rest of the evening, which left her out on a limb. With sudden determination she showered and changed out of what had been meant to be her walking clothes and went to see if the launches were still ploughing across the lake.

They were, with just an hour to go before anchoring for the night, and on impulse she boarded one that was ready to leave at any second.

As the boat cut through the water the island came into view with Libby and Nathan's house on it, and she envied them the tranquillity of the place. It was a small but very beautiful oasis amongst the grandeur of the lake and she stood looking back at it until it had disappeared from sight and the boat was stopping beside the marina at the far end where the owners of various crafts kept them moored when not in use.

As she made the return journey, which would be the last one of the day for the lake authorities, it was in the spring dusk, and calm and common sense were descending upon her. She was reading too much into a casual comment, she decided. Hugo wanting to get to know her better didn't have to mean that he wanted anything more than friendship, and if she could put his kisses to the back of her mind everything would be all right.

She'd been kissed before a few times by men and had never taken it seriously, so why not do the same now? As she put her key in the lock of the apartment it all seemed so simple to keep her problems out of the light and live each day as it came in the Lakeland paradise that she'd returned to.

The lights were on next door, she noticed. Hugo

was back early from The Mallard. Maybe like herself he needed to recharge his batteries ready for Monday morning at the surgery and she went up to bed with the tranquillity still upon her.

It lasted until Wednesday morning, with Monday and Tuesday being average sort of days and the two Lakes Rise occupants pleasantly polite to each other and re-turning home to spend the evenings separately in their own spaces.

The interview for the now vacant position of prac-tice manager that had been arranged for Gordon's niece had been scheduled for Wednesday morning at eleven o'clock and as it would be the first change of staffing since she had joined the practice Ruby was keen to get a glimpse of her.

The three senior doctors would be doing the inter-viewing as her own position was too new and junior for her to take part, so she was going to be on the lookout for Laura Armitage's arrival between patients, but she hadn't expected the consultation she was due to have with Pamela Cole, the wife of the village chemist to be so lengthy, and by the time it was over the prospective newcomer to the practice was closeted in an office on a lower level of the building with the three doctors.

Pamela had come because of finding a lump in her breast and was dreading what it might be, She had also had a recurrence of a drop in thyroid performance and Ruby had felt it necessary to increase her daily dosage of thyroxine, but the patient's only concern had been for the lump she'd found.

'I'm going to send you to the women's section of the

new hospital by the lake,' she told her. 'They will do tests there to find out the cause of the swelling, and do remember, Mrs Cole, that it isn't always cancer when that kind of thing appears. It can be from muscle strain due to heavy lifting, or some other innocent cause, so try not to worry too much until we have a diagnosis, and do make sure to take the increased dose of thyroxine that I'm going to prescribe. The hospital will be in touch with you soon, so until then just carry on as usual until you hear from them.'

When she'd gone her next patient appeared at the door of her small consulting room before she'd had the chance to call his name and as Ivor Coltrane settled himself in the chair opposite he asked, 'You're new, aren't you, and the only doctor here from the looks of it. Where are the others? They know all about my years of suffering and if they're not here I'm going to have to explain it all to you, young miss.'

'That won't be necessary, Mr Coltrane,' she told him calmly. 'I have your records in front of me. Dr Nathan Gallagher has asked for a hospital appointment with regard to your haemorrhoids, if that is what is concerning you, and you should get a letter any day. Is there anything else I can do for you, or is it just that you have come to enquire about?'

'Yes, it *was* about that,' he admitted, getting to his feet reluctantly, and she could tell that he felt he'd been denied a long chat about minor health problems that he was always eager to discuss with whichever doctor he saw.

But she'd been warned about Ivor beforehand and as

she'd explained to him, she had his notes in front of her if they should be needed, so now as he ambled slowly down the passage outside her room towards the main entrance of the practice she was free to check with one of the receptionists if the meeting was over.

'Yes,' she was told. 'They are all on their way up now. Laura's children are waiting for her in Hugo's room. We've found them some things to keep them amused and have kept popping in to make sure they were all right. One of the nurses has gone to get them.' Ruby turned at the sound of childish voices and saw a pretty girl of seven or maybe eight years old clutching the hand of a handsome younger boy. No sooner had that thought registered than those who had been at the meeting in the office downstairs came into view, with Libby and Nathan leading the way and an attractive blonde who looked to be in her middle thirties with curves in all the right places was bringing up the rear with an attentive Hugo by her side, and suddenly Ruby found herself hoping that she didn't get the job.

Surely there must be others to be interviewed before a decision was made she thought, yet this is Gordon's niece, they will give it to her because of that *and* her experience in administration in that order.

As they all came to stand in the reception area Nathan said heartily, 'Ruby is our latest recruit in the surgery, Laura, and doing a great job.' He turned to herself. 'Let me introduce Laura, our new practice manager, Ruby.' As the two women shook hands Hugo was observing Ruby's expression and wondering what was going through her mind, as it was rarely that he'd seen her so unenthusiastic about something connected with the practice.

The moment Ruby had seen the other woman a feeling of inadequacy had swept over her. She thought Laura very stylish and beautiful, and with her two lovely children, one of either sex. Just how lucky could any woman be? And it seemed Hugo had noticed her attractions too! So much for calm and tranquillity.

He walked Laura to her car, and Ruby heard him say, 'I will be only too happy to give you a lift when you move into Gordon's house, Laura. If you need help of any kind just say the word. I'm told that it could be quite some time before you join us as you're having alterations done on quite a big scale.'

She couldn't hear the other woman's reply but her smile was wide enough for it to seem that she was delighted with the offer, and deciding that she'd left her patients waiting long enough Ruby went back to them and the morning proceeded with a certain lack of lustre.

'So what's wrong?' Hugo asked, when he found her eating a sandwich in the surgery's spare car during the short break that the doctors allowed themselves for lunch. It was still her mode of transport when making house calls as it was deemed to be more suitable than the ancient Theodora for that function, and today it was somewhere to be alone for a while.

'Nothing, why?' she asked as her pulse quickened at the sight of him looking down at her through the open car window.

'You weren't exactly welcoming towards Laura, and you're eating your lunch out here?'

'So?'

'Well, why?'

What would he say if she told him she'd felt miserable because Laura had seemed to have everything that she hadn't got? Petty maybe, childish? And if for any reason Hugo should associate it with himself he might see it as the right moment for him to remind her that *she'd* made it clear that she didn't want him on *her* dating list.

'Laura seems very nice,' he said, changing the subject, 'and what cute kids. There is a marriage split somewhere according to Gordon, but obviously he didn't go into details. And listen, Ruby, if we don't get the chance to speak again before you go, I hope you have a lovely Mothering Sunday with your family this coming weekend.

'Have you got a simnel cake to take for your mother, true to the tradition down the years for children working away from home in service or something similar to be given a day off to see their mothers and present them with a cake of that sort?'

That brought a smile to her face. 'Yes. It's on order at the bakery, Hugo. I am not likely to forget that.' As the smile wavered he watched her bottom lip tremble and wondered what he'd said now to upset her.

He wasn't to know that she was trying to face up to what should have been a joyful moment, the realisation that she loved him, loved Hugo Lawrence so much she couldn't speak his name without dissolving into tenderness…and tears. She loved his thoughtfulness and his wry humour, the essential kindness of him, and his amazing attractions, but none of those things were meant for her.

As he observed them, sparkling on her lashes, he had no idea that they were because of him, he just thought how beautiful she was with her long shining swathe of hair, the coltish slenderness of her, and the big brown eyes awash with tears.

'I'm sorry if I've upset you, Ruby,' he told her softly, 'though I don't know how or why. I thought you would be looking forward to seeing your family.'

'I am,' she croaked. 'They are very special, but it isn't easy, Hugo. My mum used to be so happy but not any more.'

'Do you want to tell me about it?'

'Yes! I mean no! Definitely not! It's private!'

'All right,' he agreed soothingly, 'and now I'll leave you to finish your lunch, but remember I am always available if you need someone to talk to.'

When he'd gone she wiped away the tears with the back of her hand and munched on what was left of her sandwich unseeingly. Hugo was the last person she would want to tell that she didn't intend having children.

The weekend was pleasant enough. Her father had booked lunch for the four of them at a well-known restaurant on the Sunday, and her mother had seemed brighter than she usually was on such occasions. Possibly because Robbie hadn't had a bleed for ages,

Ruby thought, and maybe also because *she* had made no further mention of the doctor she worked with who was also her landlord.

If her mother asked about him she intended making just a casual comment about Hugo. There was no point in creating a situation that would worry the woman who had unknowingly passed on the defects of a faulty gene to the son and daughter that she loved.

As she was on the point of leaving the family home on the Sunday evening her mother said when just the two of them were together, 'You haven't mentioned your doctor friend while you've been here, Ruby.'

There was a question in the comment and she was ready with an answer. 'If you mean Hugo Lawrence, that is all he is, Mum, just a friend.'

'Remember not all men want children, Ruby. Don't punish yourself too hard,' was the reply from a mother who knew her daughter too well to accept the 'just good friends' story. It might be how the doctor felt, but there had been something in the way Ruby had spoken of him that said she had deeper feelings for him than she was prepared to admit.

'Hugo wants a house full of children,' she told her mother flatly. 'What more is there to say?' And as the rest of her family appeared at that moment to say goodbye and wish her a safe journey the brief and painful conversation came to an end.

It was past midnight when Hugo heard Theodora pull up on the drive and his brow cleared. Ruby was home safe. He was determined not to fuss and didn't intend going out to greet her, but was observing her from a side window of the house and when he saw her reaching wearily into the back seat of the car for the small overnight case that she'd taken with her he changed his mind and decided that he could at least make her a coffee and a bite after the long journey from Tyneside.

When he stepped out into the porch she turned swiftly and he said, 'Hi, there. I'm just about to have a late-night snack. Do you want to join me? You must be shattered after such a long journey.'

'I am rather,' she agreed, drowning in the pleasure of seeing him again as if they'd been separated for ever instead of just over twenty-four hours. 'Even Theodora was chugging a bit as we drove the last few miles. I would love a bite of something and a hot drink. Thanks for the offer.'

You are crazy, a voice inside her said as he stepped back to let her pass him into the elegant hallway of Lakes Rise. Where is your strength of will? You are supposed to be giving Hugo a wide berth out of work, but he has only to beckon and you come running.

She almost told him she'd changed her mind and was going to go straight to bed, but he was pointing to a chair by the last glowing embers of a log fire and moving towards the kitchen. Minutes later he reappeared with a coffee pot and slices of the ginger cake that the area was famous for and as they sat facing each other in soft lamplight he said casually, 'So did it go well, your visit back home?'

She observed him gravely, not having forgotten their

last conversation in the surgery car park where he'd found her eating her lunch inside the car.

'It was lovely,' she assured him, and it was true. The spectre that had traumatised them all for so long had been well battened down while she'd been there, and apart from those last solemn moments with her mother the atmosphere had been quite light-hearted.

Robbie had grown a lot since she'd last seen him and was now a beanstalk of an energetic teenager, her mother had smiled more than usual, and her father had been content to have her where he could see her.

'What about *your* weekend, Hugo?' she asked. 'What did *you* get up to?

He was smiling. 'I had great fun on Saturday with Toby. I took him for the day to give Nathan and Libby some quality time together, and have spent today tackling the garden here, which is sending out messages all over the place that spring is here.'

'So you had fun with Toby?' she said, trying not to sound envious. 'How did you pass the time?'

'It seems that he loves going to the island in the middle of the lake so we took the launch and a picnic lunch and were dropped off there for the day. Nathan had given us the key to the house so we could go in and out as we pleased and we had a great time exploring the place from one end to the other.'

With his voice softening he said, 'He is a fantastic kid, happy and secure with them both after losing his parents so tragically, and soon to have a little brother or sister to complete the happy family. I have to admit that I envy them.'

Not as much as I do, she thought, and wished she hadn't punished herself by asking how he'd spent what had obviously been a happy day with Toby.

Hugo was observing the changing expressions on her face.

There had been a brief rapport between them as they'd drank the coffee and eaten the cake. He'd been pleased to have her back where he could see her if not touch her. But since she'd asked how he'd spent *his* weekend the atmosphere had changed and he didn't know why.

He remembered how gentle she'd been with Toby on the night she'd looked after him so that Libby and Nathan didn't need to rush home from the party at the hotel, so surely she'd understood the pleasure that his day on the island with the child had given him?

She was getting up out of the chair, ready to go, when he asked, 'What's wrong?'

'I'm just tired, that's all,' she told him. It's been a long day and I need to get some sleep before Monday morning is upon us.'

'And that is it?' he persisted.

'Yes, that is it.' Taking his hand in hers, she held it for a moment and it was as if she'd lit a fuse.

'Don't keep doing this to me, Ruby,' he said levelly. 'I need to know once and for all if you could learn to care for me.'

Care for you! she wanted to cry. I've loved you from the moment you took me in when I was so tired and desperate for somewhere to stay. You are the most wonderful man I've ever known, and have no idea how much

I would love to give you the children you long for. But I can't bring a child into the world that might have the same blight on them that Robbie has, or be like me, a carrier of it that leaves me untouched bodily, but breaks my heart because of the bonds it binds me with.

Instead she said gravely, 'You are my best friend, Hugo, won't that do?'

'I suppose it will have to if that is all you have to offer me,' he said heavily, and as she opened the door poised for flight he went on, 'I'll see you tomorrow, Ruby…' and unaware that he was adding to her misery '…at the antenatal clinic as usual for a Monday.'

He stood and watched her walk across to her own front door and when it was safely closed behind her went slowly up to bed, telling himself as he did so that he was getting a taste of the very thing he'd vowed to avoid after witnessing his sister's grief because she'd loved *too much*. But at least Patrice had been loved in return and that must have been something to hold onto.

His was a new love that had seemed to come out of nowhere. He was happy to be Ruby's *best friend*, yet was beginning to want more than that, but she might as well be on another planet from the way she was responding to him.

CHAPTER SEVEN

I<small>T WAS</small> Easter and the village was in festive mood with garden parties on the Saturday of the weekend at various houses, including Lakes Rise, and afterwards sports on a field behind the vicarage.

Hugo had asked Ruby in the preceding week when they'd had a free moment at the surgery if she would like to host the event at his place with him and give a hand with preparing the food.

When she'd observed him warily he'd said quizzically, 'No need to panic, there are no strings attached. All those who are opening their gardens to the public will do so at ten o'clock on Saturday morning, so the first wave of visitors will be mostly there for coffee until around twelve and then it will be a light lunch available until two o'clock when the sporting activities behind the vicarage begin, and that will be it as far as Lakes Rise is concerned.

'I'll be doing a huge shop in the next few days and am planning on soup for starters, cold meats and salad for the main course, and a couple of desserts to choose from, so I would be grateful for your help if you haven't anything else planned for that day?'

She'd been smiling as he'd outlined his plans and had told him, 'Yes, of course, I'd love to help.' Her smile deepened. 'You never cease to amaze me, Hugo.'

'Why would that be?' he'd asked, refraining from commenting that it couldn't possibly be as much as *she confused him*.

"Well, this garden party for one thing. I can't envisage any other man I know offering to do that kind of thing on his own. Can you cook?'

'Of course. I wouldn't have offered if I couldn't, would I?'

'I'm sure I don't know,' she'd commented. 'The workings of your mind are a mystery to me.'

'Just as yours are to me,' he'd told her, and it had been back, the thing that lay between them, for him an unknown, unseen barrier that he wasn't allowed to cross, for her an ache that she would have for all her days and nights to come.

But not willing to let it come between them with regard to the garden party he'd said, 'So before we get sidetracked, can you be at the house for eight o'clock on Easter Saturday? And in the meantime pray for good weather for all the events being planned, as anything of that nature is always a flop if it's raining.'

They'd gone back to their respective patients after that and as the hours had ticked away Ruby had felt happier than she'd been in days. What harm could there be in them hosting together something along the lines he'd described?

For all she knew, Hugo's interest in her might be just a passing thing that would wane if he met someone else that he preferred, and irritatingly the memory of the new practice manager came to mind.

When the day dawned the sun *was* shining, the sky *was* a clear blue, and as Ruby went across to the house with a big plastic apron over jeans and a T-shirt, carrying the food that she'd prepared the night before, there wasn't a cloud in *her* sky either.

She'd awakened to the thought that she was back in Swallowbrook, and was about to spend most of the day with Hugo on a purely friendly basis. So for the moment all was well with her world and the feeling persisted all the time that the two of them were preparing the food to serve to all those whose curiosity and appetites would bring them to Lakes Rise.

Libby and Nathan were the first to arrive with Toby, and Ruby turned away from the pleasure in Hugo's expression when the boy ran up to him for a hug while his adoptive parents looked on smilingly.

'We'll have to find you a beautiful bride so that you can start a brood of your own,' Libby teased, and in the act of removing the big apron ready for serving the customers Ruby managed a pale smile.

Hugo had sensed her withdrawal and when Libby and Nathan had gone to greet others who were arriving for the garden party he asked, 'Are you all right, Ruby?'

'Er...yes,' she replied absently, as if bringing herself back from somewhere far away. 'I'm fine.' After that there was no more time for talking as there was food to serve and drinks to pour for residents and visitors to the Lakeland village on a bright sunny morning, but it didn't stop Hugo from thinking that when Ruby had

arrived at the stated time she had been even brighter
than the sun up in the sky. With eyes sparkling she'd
been ready to help him in what he'd undertaken and as
they'd laughed and joked while working side by side
he had been totally happy too.

But with the arrival of Libby, Nathan and Toby, it
was as if her light had gone out and he wondered why.
Though she was serene enough now as she helped him
to serve the food and drinks and he put his misgivings
regarding her to one side.

It was two o'clock, the garden party was over and all
was tidy after their efforts when he said, 'So are we
going to the field to take part in the sports, or do I open
a bottle of wine to toast ourselves as top-notch garden
party hosts?'

She was back on form and said laughingly, 'Oh, definitely the wine. I don't think I could even manage the
egg and spoon race after this morning's efforts, but I
did so enjoy it, Hugo.'

'Mmm,' he murmured, observing her thoughtfully,
'but not all the time, eh, Ruby? Your light went out when
Libby and Nathan turned up with Toby, didn't it? Why
was that?'

He had poured the wine and she was twisting the
stem of the glass round between her fingers as she told
him. 'It was just a silly moment, that's all, and it passed
quickly enough.'

'And you're not prepared to tell me what it was
about.'

'Er, no.'

He sighed. 'Fair enough. Maybe one day I will get to know what it is that you keep so well hidden in your past, because it can't be in your present, not the present since you arrived in Swallowbrook as I can tell that you are totally happy to be back here.'

'Yes, I am,' she agreed, and thought that coming back to the village was fantastic, but something even more wonderful than that had happened to her since her return, getting to know *him*. Still, it had its downside too as her love for him had brought the decision she'd made after genetic counselling to the forefront of every moment she spent with him, and there was no joy to be had from *that*!

'So what have you got planned for tonight?' Hugo asked as he refilled their glasses. 'There is a talent competition at The Mallard, and the biggest of the passenger launches is doing a special Easter sail of the lake with supper included. What do you think of that?'

She'd been going to say that she was having a quiet night in as it was the best way to batten down her feelings. Being close to him for so long today was weakening her resolve, but she hadn't been able to resist when he'd asked her to help with the garden party, and now Hugo was tempting her again by suggesting they sail around the lake and have supper with the sun setting on the horizon on a balmy spring evening.'

'But won't the boat be fully booked with something like that on offer?' she asked weakly.

'Maybe,' he replied, 'but I've got tickets.'

'So you were that sure I would come?'

'Pretty much, yes, because I know how you love the

lake. So is it on, Ruby, supper on the water? There will be a small orchestra on board so what more could we ask for? It's also a chance to get dressed up and let others wait on you for a change!'

It sounded wonderful, but she wasn't going to be taken for granted too easily. 'What if I've got something else planned?'

'Have you?'

'Well, no, not really, but don't expect me to fall in with everything you suggest, Hugo. It will only be the worse for you if you do.'

He was frowning. 'Those sound like words of warning.'

'Make of them what you like,' she said gravely. 'One day you might have cause to remember them.'

The frown was deepening. 'Is that a threat or a promise?'

'Neither. You were right the first time, it was a warning.'

Deciding that it was not the moment to pursue that kind of conversation, he said evenly, 'So do you want to have supper with me on the lake, Ruby?'

'Yes, please,' she told him meekly.

He was smiling now. 'So why couldn't you say so in the first place?'

'Because…'

'Because what?'

'Just because, Hugo, and now I'm going to go and search amongst my clothes for something suitable to wear, and if I can't find anything else it will have to be the red cape.'

He was laughing. 'Don't even think of it. Why don't I take you shopping and buy you something really beautiful to wear?'

'I was never meant to be beautiful,' she declared. 'I belong to the ranks of the nondescript, but I might ring the hairdresser to see if she can fit me in for a makeover before I go home to change.' And with the thought in mind she bade him a swift goodbye and went post haste down the hill to the main street of the village, leaving him wanting to tell her that to him she *was* beautiful.

When Ruby opened the door of the apartment to him that evening he took a deep breath. If she'd been appealing before, she was enchanting now. Clearly the hair salon had done as she'd asked.

The long swathe of her hair had gone. It had been shaped into a short stylish cut that showed off the contours of her face to their full advantage, the high cheek bones, the curve of the lips that he'd kissed gently on one occasion and in rising overwhelming passion on another, and the slender stem of her neck rising out of the bodice of a knee-length black dress. The dress in itself was nothing special. It was in keeping with the budget of a junior doctor. It was the woman inside it that gave it style, and he thought however much she might have attracted him before, nothing could compare to how she was affecting him now.

He sensed a change in her. The wariness she always displayed when they were together was missing, her eyes were bright, her lips parted over even white teeth. The thought came that Ruby was a creature of moods.

The one she was in tonight was most welcome, but would it last? Did he want someone who blew hot and cold all the time? But as she smiled at him with all the warmth that he wanted from her those thoughts were fleeting.

'You look very swish,' he said in a low voice as they went out onto the drive. He gazed down at the boots with the incredible heels that she'd been wearing on the night that she'd appeared in his life for the first time. 'I was going to suggest that we stroll down to the lake as it is so near, but I think maybe not.' And he opened the door on the passenger side of the car.

'I would have been fine,' she said with a smile as brilliant as the sun at midday as she swung long legs inside and settled herself in the seat, 'but if you insist…' And within seconds they were off.

If he had known the reason for the way she was glowing Hugo would have probably turned the car round and driven them back to the house, but as he didn't he carried on to the lakeside where the big launch was waiting with a festive air about it, and once he'd parked the car they went on board and were shown to their table with all the airs and graces of a top hotel.

As she looked around her Ruby was vowing to get every ounce of enjoyment out of this special night, because just for once she was going to forget about everything except the two of them, was going to pretend that she was just like other women, ordinary and without blight.

It was going to be the only time that she was going

to allow herself that pleasure. Once the night was over she would return to sanity, but not until she'd had this one wonderful evening with Hugo.

It would be time to think about the consequences when it was over. Tonight was going to be theirs, and if he ever found out why and followed Darren Fielding's example by easing himself out of their relationship, she would accept it and get on with her life as best she could.

The night was magical. As the sun sank low on the horizon the lanterns came on around the lake and while they dined a small orchestra played. One of the musicians came to tables at one point and asked the diners if there was anything special they would like them to play. When he stopped beside theirs Ruby asked for a love song that she had long adored.

'Why that?' Hugo asked softly.

'It is so beautiful,' she said dreamily, *and yearned to tell him that the words reminded her of him.*

A tear ran down her cheek. He saw it and immediately wanted to know what was wrong. It was all he seemed to do when they were together, he thought, a poor basis for the kind of relationship he wanted with Ruby, but her happiness was precious to him.

When she smiled and said, 'It was just a moment of nostalgia.' He nodded, relieved that it wasn't anything that might spoil the magic of the night.

They'd finished the meal and when the orchestra began to play the music that Ruby had asked for Hugo took her hand and led her to where part of the upper deck had been set aside for dancing.

The rest of the diners were still down below. They had the place to themselves as he took her in his arms. With the lamplit water all around them they began to dance slowly and languorously, so much in tune that it was as if the reckless mood that had taken hold of her as she'd prepared for the evening was real and everything else was a sham, when in truth it was the opposite.

Ruby was feeling the same as he did, Hugo was telling himself. She was no longer wary of him for some reason and was accepting that they belonged together. The future was opening out before him. He could see her beside him, filling the empty space in his bed for evermore, with her desire equalling his, and their children playing in the grounds of Lakes Rise with the two of them looking on fondly hand in hand.

As if she was reading his mind, she said suddenly, 'I need my wrap, Hugo, it's getting chilly out here. Shall we go back to the table?'

'Yes, of course,' he agreed evenly, aware that her mood was no longer matching his for some reason.

Ruby was panicking. She'd been crazy to think she could spend the evening with Hugo on the crest of a feeling of false euphoria born on the determination that everything in her life should be normal for once. That she should be like any other woman truly in love, honest and open, passionate and caring, but out of those things passion was the only thing she could be truthful about and that would have to last her a lifetime once she'd shut Hugo out of her life.

Aren't you making a big thing out of something small? the voice of reason was saying as they walked back to the table. They'd left it with Hugo's arm around her and returned to it as separate people. It isn't as if what you've got is catching. Yet it is, she thought, not in the usual way, but it is something that can be passed on and the wonderful man sitting opposite deserves better than that for his children.

Was it the moment to tell Hugo the reason why her moods changed so frequently while his were so constant? The words were on her lips but she couldn't say them. He hadn't asked her to marry him, or even told her he loved her, so some fool she would look if she opened her heart to him and he had no such ideas in mind, and she tried to repair what was left of the evening by saying, 'It felt really chilly out there. Maybe I should have dressed in something warmer.'

'Yes, maybe you should,' he commented in the same flat tone as when he'd agreed to her suggestion that they should break into those precious moments up on deck by going back to their table in the restaurant.

This was going to be it, he was deciding sombrely. Ruby wasn't ready for what he wanted from her, even though it had seemed that she was when she'd opened the door to him earlier and all through the evening, until now, when it was as if she'd shrunk back into her shell, and if she wasn't prepared to discuss it with him he could only draw his own conclusions.

She had turned the evening of delight into an ordeal for both of them, she thought as they wished each other a brief goodnight outside the apartment a little later, and as Hugo strode purposefully towards the house she wanted to run after him and explain about the misery and the feeling of loss that she had to live with, but could she endure watching his reaction if she did?

On Easter Sunday morning there was always a faith lunch in the village hall after the service in the church, when everyone brought an item of food, sweet or savoury, towards a buffet, and after a sleepless night Ruby decided to attend both the service and the lunch, with the thought in mind that it would shorten what was going to be a long and miserable day.

She was seated at the back of the church, waiting for the service to start with palm leaves and the heady scent of Easter lilies all around her, when Hugo appeared. As she shrank back out of sight she saw that close behind him was Laura Armstrong, the new practice manager, and her children and unbelievably the four of them seated themselves opposite.

It went without saying that Hugo was going to see *her*, she thought, wishing herself far away, but he was chatting to the children, who would shortly be enrolling at the village school, while their mother looked on approvingly, and she thought what a nice family cameo they presented.

Laura must have come to stay in Gordon's house over the weekend she decided. The repairs that she'd arranged were already under way so maybe she'd come to check on progress and to acclimatise herself with village life while she was there.

If Hugo had already known that Laura was going to be around he hadn't said anything about it while they'd been together the night before, though the reason for that might be because he'd been too occupied in writing her, Ruby, off as a non-starter when it came to love.

He looked across eventually and smiled briefly. On seeing the direction of it, Laura smiled too and Ruby knew that she was going to like the new practice manager in spite of her monopolising Hugo whenever she was around.

As the food and drink for the faith lunch were being set out after the service she asked the vicar's wife if she could help in any way and was quickly found the job of serving tea, coffee and cold drinks from a table separate from the rest, instead of being able to hide herself away in the big country kitchen where the food was being prepared, and of course the moment came when next in the queue in front of her were Hugo and the Armitage family, asking for two soft drinks and two coffees, and with colour rising she served them and wished herself far away. When the others had wandered off to find a table Hugo lingered behind and asked chattily, as if they hadn't spent the previous evening misunderstanding each other, 'How are you this morning?'

'All right, I suppose,' she replied, and continued the charade. 'How are *you*, Hugo? I see you've got company.'

'Er, yes,' he agreed absently, as if his thoughts were somewhere else. 'I met Laura and the children on my way to church and as they are strangers to Swallowbrook took them under my wing. They're here for a couple of days while she visits some of the local tradesmen to get estimates for the work she's having done, and to cast her eye upon what has been done already, but you asked if I'm all right, Ruby.

'The answer to that is I would be if I thought that you felt the same about the two of us as I do, but I'm a patient man, Ruby, I can wait.' And on that comment he went to join the Armitage family.

A short distance behind him in the queue elderly John Gallagher had been observing them and thought that their body language wasn't easy to understand. There had been no signs of disagreement about it, but neither had there been any evidence of the mutual attraction he'd seen every time he called into the surgery. So had it died a death? he wondered.

He had a feeling that he, John, might know something that the other man didn't, though he wasn't even sure of it himself. But he remembered the crisis that Ruby Hollister's family had been facing when they'd been involved in leaving the village, and how he had acted swiftly to get their toddler fast treatment in a life-and-death situation when he'd suspected he had haemophilia.

They'd moved as planned after he'd got the boy sorted and he'd sent their notes to the practice they'd registered with in Tyneside, so he'd never known the final results of the trauma except that young Robbie did have the illness and was being treated by a hospital there.

The other side of the catastrophe had been that he had a sister and there was a possibility that she would have been found to be a carrier of it, which would have put a blight on her young life too.

He didn't know if Hugo had any knowledge of what had happened to the Hollister family all that time ago, but he imagined not, and it wasn't *his* place to tell him. or interfere in any way, because of patient confidentiality, but it was food for thought, he decided with a smile for the youngest member of the surgery staff when it was his turn to be served.

When he espied Hugo with Gordon's niece and her family at a table nearby he went to join them and noted that whatever had been going on between him and Ruby, the other man's expression was giving nothing away.

While John chatted to the new family that would soon be part of the village Hugo was watching Ruby. She looked pale and tired he thought with the familiar caring feeling she aroused in him wiping out the depression of the night before.

She should be sitting here with them, relaxing. It was only yesterday that she'd been helping him at the garden party, and now she'd offered her services here.

The queue had gone and she was wiping the table down and preparing to take dirty pots into the kitchen when he reached her side and said, 'I'll do this. Pour yourself a drink and go and join John and the Armitages.'

As she was about to refuse he said, 'Don't argue, Ruby. Just do as I say. I imagine that Laura will welcome someone else to talk to after John, who talks about fishing all the time, and myself, who's having trouble concentrating on what they're saying because I've got you in view.'

She flashed him a wan smile. No doubt he was

watching her to see what she was going to do to confuse him next. But she did as he'd asked, poured herself a coffee and went to join them.

When he'd finished tidying up for her and was about to join them at the table, Ruby got to her feet and said goodbye to all of them with the excuse that she had chores to do. As she walked away Hugo thought how lost and lonely she looked and the moment it was polite enough to follow suit he went to catch her up before she got to the apartment.

But there was no sign of her walking the short distance or her already being there when he arrived at Lakes Rise. When he turned and looked towards the lake he saw a flash of the blue and white flowered dress that she'd worn for the Easter service in the church, so turning he pointed himself in that direction.

She was gazing listlessly across the calm waters when he caught up with her, and putting his concern to one side for the moment he said, 'I thought that I was the only one that you're allergic to, Ruby, but you didn't have much time to spare for the others, did you?'

'I didn't mean to be rude,' she said uncomfortably. 'It was just that Dr John was asking about my family, how they were and if they were settled in Tyneside, which reminded me of what a traumatic time it was moving from here to there, and how miserable I was to have to leave this place.'

It was a lightweight version of that time she was giving him, but when chatting to the elderly GP she hadn't been sure whether he'd been going to mention Robbie and to prevent that occurring she'd made an excuse to leave.

Hugo was looking around him beneath a darkening sky and asking, 'So what are you intending to do now?'

She shrugged slender shoulders beneath the pretty dress. 'Nothing special. I just had the urge to spend a few moments here by the lake before going back to the apartment.' She looked up into the bright blue gaze observing her. 'I'm sorry I've turned out to be such a drag on you, Hugo.

'There is nothing intentional about it, but after having to be there for your sister and her children in their distress you must feel that you've found yourself a tenant who is almost as needy.'

'Needy! That's a good one!' he exclaimed laughingly. 'You're so self-contained I can't get near you, and those black clouds in the sky are a warning that a downpour is due.'

Even as he spoke the first heavy drops were beginning to fall on them and there was nowhere to shelter along that part of the lakeside.

'Come on!' he cried, and taking her hand in his he began to run towards a distant café, but by the time they got there they were drenched.

'We can't get any wetter,' she gasped. 'Instead of standing around in wet clothes, we might as well carry on back to Lakes Rise, don't you think?'

He nodded. 'Guess you're right. Let's go.' and they didn't stop until the house came into view.

When she would have veered away towards the apartment he shook his head. 'Come to my place. I'll make us both a hot toddy when we've got into some dry clothes.' And because it would have been too painful to refuse she followed him inside without protest.

CHAPTER EIGHT

WHEN they stood dripping in the hallway and Ruby saw herself in the mirror there she exclaimed laughingly, 'What a ghastly sight! I'm soaked from head to foot, and just look at my dress.'

'I don't look much better,' he said whimsically, with the dark thatch of his hair flat against his head. She tried to lower the zip of the dress that was clinging to her like a second skin. 'Let me help you.'

He eased the zip down gently and at the same time passed her a long raincoat that was hanging on the hall stand and asked, 'Which would you prefer first, the hot drink or the shower?' Huddled in the garment that was far too big, but better than the soaking-wet dress now lying at her feet, she was beginning to shiver and. as she eased the rest of her clothes off beneath its cold folds Hugo was stripping off.

As she observed the heart-stopping masculine appeal of him, hot drinks and showers were pushed to the back of her mind. She moved towards him with lips parted and heart beating fast, with no will to resist the moment that was being presented to them, and discovered that Hugo's thoughts were not in line with hers.

Instead of reaching out for her, he said gravely, 'I've taken advantage of the moment a couple of times since we've got to know each other better, Ruby, and although it has been mind-blowing I've sensed that you have doubts about us.

'If I was to do the same again when you obviously want me to, where would we go from here? I would be taking advantage of you big time on this occasion, and by tomorrow or even later today you might be regretting it, and we can't go on like that. I want commitment from you, Ruby, and you aren't prepared to give it, are you?'

It was there again, she thought, another moment when the time might be right to tell Hugo why she couldn't do what he was asking of her, but he'd just rejected her out of hand, and mortified she picked up her wet clothes and without a word passing her lips opened the door, and squelched across to the apartment on bare feet.

You aren't thinking straight, she told herself minutes later as she lay in warm, scented water, and are making life difficult for Hugo in the process. He deserves an explanation, but can you face telling him that when you offered yourself to him tonight, it was the same as when the two of you were dancing on the boat, that both times it was because you craved to be like anyone else, free of the thing that has its hold over you?

The decisions she'd made after the genetic counselling had seemed far away on both occasions because she'd wanted him so, loved him so, and tonight had been prepared to fall into his bed and deal with any repercussions from it afterwards, she'd just wanted him to love her in return.

But she'd reckoned without Hugo's integrity and his having no knowledge of the thing that stood in the way of the commitment that he was asking from her.

When she was dressed after a long miserable soak she folded the raincoat neatly and putting it into a large carrier bag took it across to the house and placed it on the front step. Once that was done she rang the bell and made a speedy departure.

It was early evening yet seemed as if the day had been a hundred hours long and none of them enjoyable as she forced down a sandwich and tried to get interested in what was on television, but every few seconds her glance went to the house, hoping for a sight of him, and was disappointed.

The deluge that had soaked them to the skin had passed. A watery sun was struggling to get through cloud before the light went and each time she looked across there was no sign of life at Lakes Rise, although his car was on the drive.

Yet did it matter? she thought miserably. She'd spoilt what they had when she'd been so eager to offer herself to him. He'd probably gone to The Mallard to get the taste of it out of his mouth.

The prompting to go back home and find a position in general practice there was strong, but if she did that there would be nothing left of her dreams. No Swallowbrook, which meant no lake, no practice that she had always wanted to be part of, and top of the list no Hugo. Yet a voice inside her kept saying that it was the right thing to do if she was ever to have peace of mind.

Hugo had gone fell walking. The practice was closed the following day, it being Easter Monday, and in the aftermath of the fiasco when they'd arrived back drenched from the rain he'd booked in for the night at the Plateau Hotel situated on a wide ridge some distance up the nearest of the fells.

He was not happy about the way he'd treated Ruby but could see no way of putting things right between them because of her unpredictability. He dreamt all the time of making love to her in sweet nakedness. but when it had been offered to him at a cost that he knew nothing of, he'd refused.

It wasn't working, this thing between them, he'd thought bleakly as he'd walked up the first rise to where the hotel stood, and from the looks of it never would.

The place was full and noisy as the season was now getting under way. Tourists were pouring into the area either for sightseeing, walking, climbing or sailing, but he wasn't in the mood for mixing with any of them and went up to his room as soon as he'd eaten.

He would need to set off early in the morning to get to the tops and be back here for lunch, he decided as he paced the room, and should be home in the early evening, but before he turned in he had to let Ruby know where he was. Although he didn't imagine she would be keen to see *or* hear from him after the way he'd rejected her and then laid down the law with regard to what *he* would require of her.

She glanced across at the house again as the sun was setting and Ruby saw that the raincoat was still there on the front step, and as that seemed to confirm that Hugo wasn't around she went across and quickly retrieved it with the sick feeling inside that they had come to the end of their on/off relationship and if that was how Hugo felt maybe she should be grateful for a get-out.

She'd made a poor attempt at keeping within the guidelines of the promises she'd made to herself when they'd both been on the verge of nakedness and from now on was not going to put a foot wrong. But as the night wore on with still no sign of life at the house she couldn't settle until the phone rang at nine o'clock and his voice came over the line.

'Ruby, it's me,' he said abruptly. 'I'm at the Plateau Hotel halfway up Stone Wall Fell, if anyone needs me for anything. I'm going to carry on to the top in the morning and should be back at Lakes Rise by early evening tomorrow at the latest.'

'Yes, I see. Take care, Hugo, and thanks for letting me know,' she replied woodenly, and thought surely he didn't have to go to such lengths to get away from her.

He was as good as his word and came striding up the drive early Monday evening, just minutes after she'd been across to the house once more and deposited the raincoat with its painful memories on the front step.

Hugo glanced across at the apartment briefly and as

she was nowhere in his line of vision he bent and picked up the raincoat and went inside and she thought miserably that it was over almost before it had begun, the love affair that hadn't had a chance from the start, and if he found that hard to believe he would soon change his mind when she gave in her notice tomorrow.

During the last twenty-four hours she had decided that although it would be heartbreaking, it was the best thing to do. She would go home to her family where her problem was no secret, where she didn't have to pretend and watch what she did, and maybe one day Hugo would find someone who would be ready to give him the children that he would want. She could never begrudge him that.

Now that the decision had been made she felt calmer, less distraught because she was keeping to the path that she'd chosen to follow, and she could only do that if he wasn't around.

She would be expected to work a month's notice, which was part of her contract and might be awkward with them living so near each other, but there was no reason why they should be in each other's company more than needs be at the surgery and when she came home she would go in and shut her door and hopefully the time would soon pass.

Once again there was no sign of him when she was ready to leave for the surgery on Tuesday morning and she breathed a sigh of relief. The last thing she wanted was to confront him with the weight of what she was about to do heavy on her mind. As she settled herself behind the wheel of her car she said sadly, 'It's going to be just you and me again, Theodora. What do you think about that?' And with a splutter and a roar they were off.

'This *is* a surprise, Ruby!' Libby exclaimed when she gave in her notice.

And Nathan commented, 'We thought you were happy here as part of the practice?'

'I was, I am,' she said awkwardly. 'It is a private matter that has caused me to offer my resignation.'

'I see, and you will be working your month's notice, I hope?'

'Yes, of course,' she told him, and Libby thought how pale she was, this clever, likeable young doctor, and wondered if her leaving the practice was anything to do with Hugo, who had just pulled up outside the surgery after doing a house call on his way there. She'd seen them together a few times and sensed there was chemistry between them.

Ruby had gone to her room and was already seeing her first patient when he came striding in, and when they told him that she was leaving he gazed at them slack-jawed.

'Since when?' he wanted to know.

'Since just five minutes ago,' Nathan told him.

'Did she say why?' he asked tightly.

'Just that it is for personal reasons,' Libby explained, hoping he might have some answer to the surprising news, but if he had Hugo wasn't saying anything and stayed chatting about other things for a while longer before going to sort out his patients of the day and left the other two doctors to do likewise.

As he closed the door of his consulting room behind him he groaned out loud. The situation between Ruby and himself had been bad enough over the weekend but this was something else! She was leaving the place she loved and it was because of him, he thought grimly.

What was he supposed to do, let her? She would be working the standard notice period, no doubt, so there would be just a month before life lost its meaning and in that time he had to find the answer that he sought.

It was always extra-busy at the practice after a long weekend such as the Easter one and today was no exception. There was no break for lunch, the staff were all having a bite while working, which left no opportunity for him to talk to her, and in any case, surrounded by others like him who would also be surprised that her time with them was going to be so short, did he want to air his frustrations in public?

Each time they came face to face in the surgery Ruby turned away, not willing to meet his glance, and by the time their working day was over he was consumed with impatience.

She was home before him. Nathan had wanted a brief chat before they separated at the end of the day with regard to Ruby's news of the morning, in the hope that he, Hugo, might be able to throw some light on the surprise announcement. But there was no way he was going to bring his private life into the open, no matter what, and though he'd sympathised with the other man's dilemma he'd thought that it was nothing compared to his own and they'd separated, each with his own questions regarding Ruby.

When he arrived at Lakes Rise the door at the bottom of the stairs that led to the apartment was open and he called, 'Can I come up?'

There was a faint 'Yes' from above and he wasted no time.

She was standing in front of the cooking range, listlessly tossing a pancake in the air every few seconds, and if he hadn't been so stressed he would have laughed at the absurdity of the moment, yet even so he couldn't resist saying, 'Shrove Tuesday has been and gone, the same as you have in mind for yourself, Ruby. Why on earth have you decided to leave the place that you love? The job you love? If it's because of me I promise to stay away from you. Our relationship got lost somewhere along the way, didn't it, yet it doesn't mean that you have to do anything as drastic as giving in your notice.'

She could have told him, *Yes, I do love Swallowbrook, I do love the job, but I love you more and as far as I can see I won't be bringing you much joy if I stay.*

Instead she said, 'I'm sorry, Hugo. I've made up my mind. I'm going home and will find myself a position there.'

'You do know you're letting the practice down, I suppose?' he commented, trying another approach. 'Libby will be leaving soon because of the baby, and now you're going, which will leave us two doctors short.'

Her resolve was weakening. Another second of having to listen to his calm reasoning and it would be so easy to change her mind, but Hugo didn't know the worries that consumed her and if in the future he should ever discover her reasons for behaving the way she had, her mood swings and the way she'd offered herself to him in a moment of indescribable longing and been refused, he might feel that he'd had a lucky escape.

'Will you please go?' she said, switching off the hotplate and depositing the dishevelled pancake in the waste bin. 'I need to phone my parents to tell them that I'm coming home to live.'

'Yes, of course,' he said evenly. 'I hope they tell you that you're crazy for letting a few misunderstandings uproot you from Swallowbrook for a second time.' And before she could reply to that he'd gone.

The days were long after that with Hugo keeping to his promise and staying away from her except when on surgery business, and as the evenings dragged on with her overwhelmingly conscious of him in the house across the way, so near yet so far, Ruby sought solace by the lake, either sailing on it, sitting by it or walking beside it.

Spring would soon be making way for summer, she thought frequently, and where would she be then? Job hunting back on Tyneside, or on the dole if all the cuts in health care that were being threatened took place, and it would all be for the sake of a clear conscience.

Yet it wasn't *that* clear. It would only be completely so if she confessed to Hugo the reason for her strange behaviour, but the thought of the look on his face if she told him didn't bear thinking of, having to observe the dismay and pity there would break her heart.

The first week of her notice had passed with few comments from the surgery staff but no shortage of strange looks. Yet the patients had no qualms about saying what they thought and one morning Hugo said, 'Nathan wants me to take you with me when I go to visit Sarah Bellingham. She's just come out of hospital after a serious hip operation and is causing problems for the district nurse because she keeps refusing to have the prescribed injections of antibiotics into the stomach area to prevent infection.

'In some cases it's the standard thing, while in others it's done intravenously, but Sarah is not the type to be on a drip or tubed up in any way.

'Apparently you did a house call to her shortly after you joined the practice. She liked you and remembered you from when you lived here before, so we're hoping you can charm the old lady into letting the nurse do what she has to do.'

It was the first time they'd been anywhere together since she'd handed in her notice and every moment was precious because there wouldn't be many of them to treasure in the next few weeks.

After listening to what he had to say, she told him, 'Yes, I went to see Mrs Bellingham when I first came here. She had a chest infection and was too frail to come to the surgery as her mobility isn't very good, for one thing, but her mind is clear enough.' And thought it must be if she'd remembered her from all that time ago.

As Hugo stopped the car in front of a typical lake-land cottage she hoped that it had been only her face that the old lady had remembered and nothing else from way back.

The district nurse, who had arrived before them, was waiting at the gate and when the three of them appeared in the sitting room the patient was sitting by the window with the leg that had been operated on in a raised position on a footstool.

When she saw them she said, 'So Nathan Gallagher has sent reinforcements to pin me down while I have the needle, has he?'

Ruby stepped forward, took a frail hand in hers, and said gently, 'Even big strong men have been known to go pale at the sight of a needle, Mrs Bellingham, so you aren't alone in the way you feel, but you've just come through major surgery and all of that could be thrown into chaos if you get an infection, so you do need to allow Nurse to give you the injection.'

'Yes, all right,' she agreed reluctantly, 'as long as you keep holding my hand, but before the nurse starts sticking the needle in me I've been wondering how that young brother of yours is. Wasn't he poorly when you lived here before?'

Hugo had been watching the scene before him with a sickening feeling of loss as he'd observed Ruby's gentle approach to the elderly woman's problem, and it wasn't just his own loss that he was contemplating with her departure. There was the loss to the practice too that would result from her decision to leave the village, so with those thoughts in mind he didn't tune in to the way she'd tensed at the question.

But her smile didn't falter as she replied. 'Yes, Robbie *was* poorly, Mrs Bellingham, but he's fine now.'

It was a half-truth, but the extent of it wouldn't matter one way or the other because soon she would be gone, taking her problems with her, but the patient had more to say and this time it was with regard to her leaving the practice.

'They tell me that you're leaving us, which seems a bit odd as you haven't been here long,' she went on to say. 'I hope you're not one of these young folk who only care about themselves.'

'No, I'm not, far from it, but sometimes a situation arises that we have no control over, Mrs Bellingham, and that is how it is with me,' she told her without meeting Hugo's glance, and as the nurse was waiting to give the injection the subject was closed.

But only until the two doctors were back in the car and as Hugo was about to speak she forestalled him by saying, 'I know what Mrs Bellingham said about my leaving is what people are thinking and you especially, Hugo, but my life is my own to do as I will with it, and what I'm doing at the present is the right thing, believe me.'

'You're telling me that,' he said with brows rising, 'when I'm trying to grope my way through your thought processes like a man in a fog. I think Sarah might have hit the nail on the head when she questioned your motives.'

'I can't bear to quarrel with you,' she said wretchedly. 'If we can't be lovers, can't we at least be friends?'

'You mean as pen pals?' he questioned dryly. 'I can't see it being anything else with all the miles that will be between us.'

He was pulling onto the forecourt of the practice and adding to her dejection said, 'If you still want to carry on with the charade that we're both involved in and the apartment is going to be vacant, I suppose I could offer it as a temporary residence to Laura and her family when you've left. It would be somewhere for them to stay while the refurbishment of Gordon's house is taking place.' And with that final nail in the coffin of her dreams she opened the car door and was out in a flash, hurrying inside before anyone should witness her distress.

Hugo banged the steering-wheel in frustration; he was totally screwing this up! There was just three weeks to go before Ruby went out of his life and during that time he had to make her see that they were meant to be together, that she was his bright morning star, and Sarah Bellingham's suggestion that she was being selfish wouldn't have helped much towards that end.

The day progressed like any other, patients coming and going for both the doctors and the nurses, with the exception of Nathan popping in to compliment Ruby on the way she'd handled Sarah, and in the lunch hour Libby commenting how pale and drawn she looked and asking if she was all right while the two of them were lunching in the surgery kitchen.

'Yes, I'm fine,' she was assuring her, and at that moment there was a voice from the doorway.

'If ever you want a chat, Ruby, I'm always available.'

When she'd looked up John Gallagher was standing there and she'd wondered how much he knew about her family's last days in the village.

When Ruby arrived home that evening there were flowers waiting for her at the entrance to the apartment, a beautiful bouquet of lilies of the valley and pink roses with a card attached that said, 'Please forgive me my negative attitude this morning, Ruby. I'll be by the lake at eight o'clock in the place where we got rained on if you'd like to hear my apology in person.'

As she arranged the flowers lovingly in a crystal vase that graced the centre of the dining table, the thought was there that he was a generous man, willing to put her needs before his own because all he was getting out of knowing her was frustration.

Why hadn't Hugo suggested that he would come to the apartment to speak to her, she wondered, instead of them meeting by the lake? It would be more private, yet did she want that? If he so much as touched her she would be lost and that wasn't likely to happen amongst the crowds down there, so was she going to go? Yes, she was. If only to tell him that no apology was needed.

She'd washed the blue and white dress of the day of the downpour and was tempted to wear it, but common sense warned her not to make too big a thing of the occasion. She could be back within minutes, which might be a good idea under the circumstances, and as the evening sun looked warm and inviting she put on a cotton shift dress and open sandals, and at a quarter to eight walked down to where he had suggested they meet.

It was crowded down by the lakeside, as she'd expected, yet Hugo stood out amongst them as he gazed across to where the windows of Libby and Nathan's house on the island glinted in the sun and a launch full of sightseers was cutting its way through the water en route to the moorings.

How could it be that someone like Hugo should want *her*? Some other woman with no faulty genes would soon be there in the foreground when she'd gone and why not? Hugo deserved someone better than her to share his life.

When he turned he had no smile for her, just a grave nod above the heads of those milling around them, and he asked, 'Shall we find somewhere less crowded?'

'Yes, if you like,' she agreed, and as they walked to where there was an empty seat in a secluded corner beside ancient crags that had been there for ever she took the opportunity to say, 'Thank you for the flowers, Hugo. No one has ever done that for me before. They are really beautiful, and before you say anything, I don't need an apology from you because you haven't done anything wrong.'

He was smiling now and as she watched it transform his face he said, 'So dare I ask something of you instead?'

'Er, yes,' she agreed uneasily.

'Will you marry me, Ruby?' he said softly. 'Will you

put your trust in my making you happy and contented as we build a future together with our children? Can you put to one side your uncertainties of recent weeks and be my wife? We could have such a good life together in this beautiful place.'

She had often wondered how she would cope if this moment ever arose, and as her mouth went dry and she began to shake, now she knew.

'Is that really what you brought me down here for?' she croaked, 'or is it just a spur-of-the-moment kind of thing?'

'It is something I've wanted to say to you almost from the moment we met, but there has never been the right moment, and judging from your expression it would seem that still applies. Does it?' he asked, and now his voice was flat and remote as he observed her dismay.

'I'm not intending having children, Hugo. They are not included on the agenda of *my* life as they are on yours,' she told him lifelessly. 'So the answer has to be no. I've seen you with little ones at the surgery and with young Toby and you'll make a fantastic father when the right person comes along.'

'So you don't love me?' he questioned bleakly.

'I didn't say that. Shall we just say I'm not in the market for bringing children into the world, while you are, and the two don't mix?'

'And that is why you're leaving?' he said incredulously.

'I don't think we need go into that. I'm honoured to know that you should want me as your wife but, as

Sarah Bellingham suggested, maybe I'm one of the self-ish young generation who want it all their own way.'

With tears threatening she looked up at him and said, 'If you will excuse me, Hugo, I feel that this conversation has gone on long enough.'

As he was about to protest she touched his lips fleetingly with her fingers and shook her head, then began to walk slowly in the direction of Lakes Rise and the apartment, not daring to turn in case she weakened in her resolve and went back to where she wanted to spend the rest of her life, in his arms.

CHAPTER NINE

STILL reeling from Ruby's blunt, almost brutal rejection of his proposal Hugo caught her up as she was putting her key into the lock of the apartment in a sudden desperate rush to be on her own after having done the thing that she'd dreaded doing so often to a man of her dreams, saying no when he asked her to marry him.

Heartbreakingly it had been Hugo that she'd had to hurt, Hugo that she had fallen in love with deeply and abidingly. Hugo who wanted children from a marriage, which was perfectly understandable, and she hadn't been able to face telling him why she couldn't give them to him.

Instead she'd told him flatly that marrying him wasn't what she had in mind for both their sakes and had left him to digest *that*, when every word had felt as if she would choke on it, and now he was here, wanting answers, no doubt, and she hadn't got any unless she told him the unpalatable truth that if she gave him children they might either be haemophiliacs or carriers of the gene.

'Hold on a moment,' he said as the door swung back to let her in, and as she gazed at him, eyes wide and anxious. 'I asked you down there by the lake if you don't want to marry me because you don't love me, but you denied that, so what is it all about, Ruby?'

'I told you, Hugo,' she said wearily, as the futility of the moment took hold of her even more. 'Our wishes for the future are not compatible so please go and leave me alone.'

'I'm going, have no worries on that score,' he said flatly. 'If you don't want children, you don't. But I can't remember making that a condition of my proposal. Perhaps I should point out that I'm not looking for a breeding machine. I would just want to have a couple of youngsters with the woman I love and a happy family life.

'I've hoped all along that deep down you wanted me as much as I wanted you, which was foolish of me, I suppose, and I should be grateful that you are letting me off the hook now, instead of me continuing to think along those lines.'

On that last comment he went and she closed the door behind her and went slowly up to bed with the words they'd exchanged going round in her head like a runaway carousel.

It was done, she thought as sleep eluded her. She'd found the strength to send Hugo out of her life. All she had to do now was exist without him and with that thought the tears came, running down her cheeks and soaking the pillows.

In Lakes Rise just a few feet away, where he'd dreamt of living with Ruby and their little ones, Hugo was also relinquishing his dream and deciding that for the next three weeks it was going to be hell on earth until Ruby left Swallowbrook. After that he couldn't bear to think about, but the fact remained that she didn't want to marry him.

The lifestyle that he had wanted for them both had not been the same as hers and he was still stunned to know she didn't want children. But in any relationship it was the woman who had to go through the pain and the invasion of her body to bring children into the world, so she should have the right to say yes or no to having a family. Though he sensed with regard to Ruby it wasn't like that. She just didn't want *him* or *his* children.

So where did they go from here? he wondered as he gazed across at the apartment that was all in darkness. She'd been so definite about her feelings he just had to let her go, but in the short time that was left before her departure he had to find an answer of some sort for her reasoning.

She hadn't given him the chance to talk through the bombshell that she'd thrown at him, but before the next three weeks were up he hoped that the answer he sought would come from somewhere, otherwise he would spend the rest of his life in a state of miserable limbo.

After observing the extent of his sister's grief at the loss of the husband she'd adored he had vowed never to leave himself wide open to that kind of heartache, the pain of those who loved too much, yet here he was, devastated, not because of a bereavement—Ruby was very much alive and well—it was the death of his hopes and his dreams that was making life seem so meaningless.

For Ruby the rest of the week was an ordeal to be got through with Hugo politely aloof whenever they had to communicate at the surgery and nowhere to be seen in the evenings.

She was grateful for the challenges that each day brought with regard to the job, such as when a pregnant woman who would soon be giving birth came to see her with a bladder problem that she was frantic might harm the baby in some way. An on-the-spot urine test showed blood there without there being any signs of cystitis or something similar, and when the patient had experienced great difficulty in producing even the smallest amount to be tested, she had sent for an ambulance immediately and told her that the surgery would get in touch with relatives to explain what was happening and would suggest that they go straight to A and E.

Then there had been a man from the Forestry Commission who had cut his leg with a saw and got an infection in the wound, which had meant a prescription for antibiotics and antiseptic dressings in the nurses' room.

His problem had been more run of the mill than that of the pregnant woman, but needed to be watched nevertheless. Her pregnant patient had been diagnosed as having too much pressure on the bladder from a large foetus and she would have to stay in hospital until the birth if the baby didn't change its position and its weight become more evenly balanced.

There had been no mention so far of the other doctors seeking someone to fill the gap that she was going to leave, and she wondered if Libby and Nathan were expecting her to change her mind at the last moment. She knew there were no such thoughts coming from Hugo, but he was better informed than they were with regard to her reasons for leaving.

It was Friday again, the last working day of what had been a dreary week as far as she was concerned, and in the evening a yearly event was taking place in the assembly hall of the village school, the play that the staff and their young pupils presented after much hard work to parents and friends.

She knew that Hugo had been taking it for granted that the two of them would be going together to see Toby in his first school play and he'd bought tickets a couple of weeks ago, but that had been before he'd asked her to marry him and their relationship had foundered.

Now all the tickets had been sold and she'd given up on the idea of going until on arriving home from the surgery on the Friday evening she found the ticket that he'd got for her on the mat when she opened the door and as she'd stared down at it she decided that she was going to go.

It wasn't numbered so she didn't have to sit next to Hugo, she told herself as she bent to pick it up. There would be lots of folk there. They might not even get a glimpse of each other in the packed hall, but that was what she wanted, wasn't it?

Having felt like a drab all week, she put on the blue and white dress and spent extra time on hair and make-up. But when she stepped in front of a long mirror in the bedroom before walking down to the school she was asking herself why was she was dressing up. There would be no one she wanted to impress at the play. Hugo was out of her life for good, she'd been too cruel and outspoken for him to want to have anything to do with her ever again.

As was sometimes the case with the best-laid plans they went astray and the moment Ruby entered the place she saw Libby waving from a row near the front with Nathan on the one side and Hugo on the other. She was pointing to the empty seat next to him and beckoning her across to sit with them, and short of being down-right rude there was nothing she could do but join them.

As she seated herself next to him Libby said, 'Hugo is here at Toby's request. Who have you come to clap for, Ruby?'

She was so aware of him sitting silently beside her she could hardly breathe, but with bright colour staining her cheeks managed to say, 'Er, all of them, I suppose. I used to be a pupil here myself.'

'And did your brother attend this school too?' Nathan questioned casually. 'I don't seem to remember him.'

'You won't,' she told him. 'Robbie was just a toddler when we left Swallowbrook. There is quite a difference in our ages.'

So far Hugo hadn't spoken, but now he broke his silence to ask, 'Are you packed up and ready to leave in a couple of weeks' time?'

'More or less,' she told him, knowing that she'd never been less ready for anything than she was for her departure from Swallowbrook, but with peace between them she would just about manage to get through the days that were left if there were no further discussions, or touching, or false rapport, and then it would be back to Tyneside and the rest of her life without him.

The play was over, the young performers had taken their bows and while Libby and Nathan went to find Toby behind the scenes Ruby and Hugo were left to wait for them in an uncomfortable silence that seemed neverending until at last they appeared and as usual Toby came running straight to Hugo and he swung him up into his arms and held him close.

Ruby turned away. It was how he would be with children of his own, she thought achingly. They would be blessed to have Hugo as a father, but there would be no blessings coming their way if *she* was their mother.

He had watched her turn away and it had brought back the hurt that had never left him since she'd refused to marry him, but he wasn't going to open up that raw wound again. If Ruby had told him she didn't love him he would have accepted it, but she hadn't said that. She'd as good as admitted that she *did* love him, but not enough to marry him and have his children.

Libby and Nathan were spending the weekend as they often did at their house on the island and were intending sailing across in their motor launch as soon as the play was over, so there was no cause for Ruby and Hugo to linger, and after they'd all said their goodnights

Ruby found herself walking back to the apartment with him and the silence that had been between them as they'd waited for Libby and Nathan to find Toby backstage was back again, until they reached Lakes Rise and as she was about to make a quick getaway he held out his hand in front of her and on the palm of it was a small jeweller's box.

Mesmerised and shaken, she thought frantically, Please don't ask me again, Hugo. I won't be able to say no a second time. But she'd got it wrong. He had no intention of doing any such thing. Instead he lifted the lid and as she gazed wide-eyed at a ruby glowing red in a bright gold setting, he said, 'As this is no longer of any use to me, you might as well have it. Do what you want with it, Ruby, I don't mind.' And leaving her totally speechless he went, bypassing the house so that she would have no chance to catch him up to refuse, or enthuse over the ring, and straight to The Mallard where the conversation would be mundane and easy to handle.

Ruby sat and gazed at the ring with the glowing stone that she was named after for hours after he'd gone and with every passing moment knew she wasn't going to give it back to Hugo. It was a beautiful thing that he would have chosen with his hopes high, expecting to put it on her finger when he'd asked her to marry him, and now it meant nothing to him.

But to her it would be something to remind her of the only man she would ever love, the one who had taken her to his heart and awakened her dormant passions, cared for her when she was weak and lost on her first night back in Swallowbrook, and now she had something to remember him by that she would always wear. Not on her finger, she had no right to do that, but on a slender gold chain around her neck, unseen by others. Only she would know it was there and be comforted.

Since she had rung home to say she was coming back to Tyneside there had been mixed feelings in the family. There was pleasure because they would see more of her. Robbie was especially delighted while knowing nothing of the circumstances, because 'big sis', as he called her, was coming back to live with them.

But there was also anxiety because both her parents knew something that the man who wanted to marry her didn't, and they ached for their daughter.

Her mother was very quiet with only Ruby's one cryptic comment about Hugo Lawrence's love of children to go by with regard to the end of the love affair, and knowing how the reason for it would hurt the woman who had given birth to her, she'd made light of it on the night that she'd phoned to say she was coming back home to live, which left Jess not knowing what to think.

But not so her father. He knew his daughter too well not to pick up on the sadness in Ruby that she'd been quick to deny on the occasions when he'd phoned her since she'd said she was leaving Swallowbrook, and he had drawn his own conclusions.

After the gift of the ring Ruby was consumed with the urge for it to be as near to her heart as possible and the next morning, taking advantage of it being Saturday, she drove into the town to the main jeweller's on the high street whose name was on the box that it had been in and bought the chain that would hold the ring warm and safe between her breasts.

After a coffee in a nearby café she was preparing to drive back to the village when she saw Laura Armitage and her children also out shopping, if the number of bags and parcels they were carrying was anything to go by.

As the two of them stopped to pass the time of day the woman who was shortly to take over the practice manager position that her uncle had left vacant said, 'We've just seen Hugo chatting to Libby and Nathan with Toby in one of the stores and now we see you, Ruby. The Swallowbrook doctors must have all had the same idea this morning.'

Not exactly, Ruby thought. They might have all come to shop, but she would be the only one who had come to buy a chain for a ring that she was going to wear around her neck when its rightful place was on her finger.

'Where exactly did you see them, Laura?' she asked the other woman, who pointed vaguely in the direction of a new store that had just opened, which prompted Ruby to go in the other direction as they each went their separate ways

She had reckoned without the long arm of coincidence that sometimes reached out when least expected, and while she was filling the petrol tank at a garage on the way back to the village Hugo's car pulled in behind her and he came to stand beside her as she was replacing the petrol cap.

He was smiling in spite of what was going on in their lives. Just the sight of her was enough to brighten his day. 'It seems as if we've all had the same idea, to do an early shop,' he said. 'Libby and Nathan were in one of the stores, and Laura and her family appeared while I was chatting to them.'

A casual glance inside the car and his smile disappeared. He'd seen the fancy bag with the jeweller's name on it that contained the chain and she thought with sick dismay, *Surely he doesn't think I've changed the ring for something else. Please don't let it be that!*

Yet she couldn't ask him if it was, it would be just too awful if she was wrong and totally horrific if she was right. With all speed she went to pay for the fuel and while Hugo was busy at the pumps wished him a brief goodbye and drove off.

The rest of the weekend was going to be an exercise in depression that would make past days seem joyful if she didn't explain to Hugo about the chain. There was no need for Hugo to know why she'd bought it, but clear the air she must for the sake of her peace of mind…and his.

But time passed and when there was no sign of him coming back to the house her anxiety regarding the bag from the jeweller's switched to his whereabouts, which unknown to her were connected with him having clothes for fell walking and other equipment in the boot of his car, and an arrangement with the mountain

rescue services that he could be contacted at short notice in an emergency.

A group from a nearby sixth form college had gone
on a supervised walk up one of the fells and got lost in
thick mist up on the tops, so much so that instructions
for them all to stay together hadn't been as easy to ad-
here to as had been thought, and now it was chaos up
there, with small groups trying to find their way down
in very poor visibility. Others were wisely staying put
until it improved.

Along with other experienced fell walkers Hugo and
Nathan had both received calls to turn out with a team
of mountain rescue volunteers and if Ruby had known
that she might have felt that her urgency for Hugo's
company came a poor second to the needs of the lost
teenage walkers, but as she didn't, it wasn't until Libby
phoned in the early evening to explain his absence that
she became aware that on this occasion the needs of
others had to come first.

Another call from Libby at the cottage much later in
the evening was to say that the lost and those who had
gone to bring them down to safety were all back at the
village hall being given warm drinks and blankets to
bring up body temperatures. Though it had been a mild
day by the lakeside it had been very cold on the tops,
and her last item of information before she rang off was
to say, 'Hugo's car has just gone past. He should arrive
at Lakes Rise any moment, Ruby,' and as she replaced
the receiver he was pulling up on the drive.

When he got out of the car he looked tired and drawn

and she was beside him in a flash, all else forgotten in the need to cherish him for a few precious moments.

'Would you like some supper?' she asked. 'I've made a quiche and a salad, with blueberry crumble and custard to follow.'

'To what do I owe the honour?' he asked quizzically.

'Two reasons,' she told him, 'firstly because it can't have been very pleasant up there tonight.'

'True,' he agreed. 'And what's the second?'

'That I've been waiting for hours to explain what the bag from the jewellers was doing in my car.'

'Why do you feel you have to do that?'

'Because I thought you might have wondered if I'd been to exchange the ring you gave me for something else.'

'And had you?'

'No! Of course not! I would never do such a thing.'

'Good. I'm glad to hear it, though does it matter?'

Yes, it does, it really does, she thought wistfully, achingly aware of the glowing jewel hidden from sight, and bringing her thoughts back to the reason why they were having this conversation at close on midnight, she said, 'So are you going to come and join me for supper?'

'Er, yes of course,' was the reply. 'It's kind of you to offer. Give me a few moments to get changed and cleaned up and I'll be with you.' He strode across to the house and disappeared from sight and she went back into the apartment to wait for him with the knowledge that she wasn't any wiser regarding what Hugo had thought when he had seen the bag from the jeweller's in the car, but at least she'd explained the reason for it in an oblique sort of way from her point of view.

It would have put her mind at rest if she'd known that he hadn't thought anything in particular when he'd seen it. It had been merely a matter that observing the familiar name on the bag had reminded him of the fate of the ring that he'd bought with high hopes of seeing it on her finger, and instead had ended up giving it to her as a sign of defeat.

And now as she waited for him the thought was there that this might be the last time they shared a meal, were together on their own, and she couldn't bear it, but if Hugo picked up on her distress it would bring them into the kind of situation that they always ended in, heart searching and half-truths from her side, and she didn't want that tonight.

The table was set for two in soft lamplight when he appeared looking scrubbed and clean after scrambling around the fells searching for the lost ones who would now be homeward bound in the coach that had brought them to Swallowbrook.

To his amazement she'd changed into the blue dress that he'd once asked her to wear and had seen the request ignored. Was there a message in that, or had it just been the first thing she'd seen in the wardrobe? he wondered.

There was just a week to go before Ruby disappeared out of his life and tonight was the only time he'd felt any closeness between them since she'd flatly refused to marry him, and even now it could be just wishful thinking on his part.

It could be that she was doing what any friend would do for him after a pretty gruelling day, making him a meal and giving him the pleasure of her company, but it didn't explain the blue dress, and he wasn't going to ask why tonight of all nights she was wearing it. She'd been dressed in jeans and a sweatshirt when she'd come out onto the drive to speak to him when he had arrived home.

If it *was* a good omen and Ruby was changing her mind about leaving the village, the practice, *and him,* she was going to have to make the first move. He'd been down that road once and had been groping for an answer to what was going on in his life ever since.

She was crazy, thought Ruby as she dished the food out in the apartment's small kitchen. In the last three weeks she'd kept her distance from Hugo except for at the surgery, and now tonight when it was almost time for her to go she was melting with love for him, aching for him to make love to her just once so that she would have something to hold onto in the dark days of a future without him.

But she'd seen the look in his eyes when he had noticed the dress and it hadn't been pleasure there. Just a wary, questioning sort of look that said, *Don't play games with me, Ruby.* If it wasn't for the fact that it would be so obvious she would dash into the bedroom and change back into the jeans and cotton top.

Unaware of the thoughts going round in her head Hugo smiled when she put the food in front of him and said, 'I can't remember the last time someone made a meal for me.'

'What about your sister?' she asked

'It was more a matter of me doing the cooking when she was here. Patrice had no interest in anything, until she was suddenly taken with the idea of living in Canada near a friend who'd come over on a visit. Before I knew it she'd gone and I was free to live my own life, until on a winter's evening a vision appeared in a red cape…'

She was laughing. 'Please don't bring that up again. I shudder when I think about the way I blundered into your ordered life.'

'And now you're going out of it as quickly as you came into it.' he said, sombre now, 'and I still don't understand.'

'It's better if you don't,' she told him in a low voice. 'A lot of things are best that way.'

'Not when they concern the two of us, Ruby,' he said tightly. 'Don't insult my intelligence.'

She had seated herself opposite and after that there was silence between them until they'd finished the meal. When she went into the kitchen to make coffee he followed her and doing the very thing that he'd vowed not to do said, 'Why the blue dress? Or is it something else that I'm better off not knowing?'

'I put it on because I thought it might be our last time alone. I'm going home at the end of next week, probably driving to Tyneside on the Sunday evening, and remembering how you'd once asked me to wear it and I didn't, I thought that it might make up for it a little.'

'And that's it?'

'Yes, more or less.'

'And suppose I asked you to go one step further and slip out of it, the same as you were going to do with the raincoat when we'd got caught in the downpour that time? Would you do that for me to make up for me being so slow to respond then?'

'No,' she said softly. 'The desire is there, urgent and compelling. I've wanted to give myself to you since the moment you arrived, but it would be like leaving us with unfinished business if we made love during my last few days in the village. I would want more and it wouldn't be right.'

'So we're still playing guessing games,' he said dryly. 'I'll skip the coffee if you don't mind, Ruby. Thanks for the meal, it was most welcome. Enjoy what's left of the weekend and I'll see you Monday.'

Before she could cave in to the temptation to forget everything except how much she wanted him, he had gone and she was left to imagine what life would be like without Hugo living just a few yards away.

On the Monday morning they were both in for a surprise. Libby and Nathan were arranging a small dinner party at the house on the island for the coming weekend with John Gallagher and themselves as guests.

When Nathan mentioned it to Hugo before the surgery got under way on the Monday morning his spirits lifted. If Ruby accepted the invitation it would give them a little more precious time together in beautiful surroundings, he thought, with his good friends the Gallaghers to make it complete.

It was Libby who passed on the invitation to Ruby, who had just arrived at the practice looking downcast, and as she watched her hesitate the thought came that the young doctor who had been with them for so short a time was going to refuse and the whole idea of the friendly little get-together would be wasted, as she and Nathan had thought of it as a last opportunity for two people they liked and respected to get their lives sorted in tranquil surroundings.

But Ruby was smiling, the colour was coming back into her cheeks.

'I'd love to come, Libby,' she said. 'My last two days here by the lake will be more bearable with that to look forward to.'

CHAPTER TEN

'HAVE you accepted Libby and Nathan's invitation to their dinner party on your last weekend here?' Hugo asked when he and Ruby came face to face at the end of morning surgery.

'Yes,' she replied, with the memory of his abrupt exit from the apartment the night before still clear in her mind. 'Have you?'

'Of course,' he replied. 'An overnight stay on the island with friends is something I wouldn't want to miss. John has suggested that the three of us sail over together on Saturday afternoon, if that's all right with you.'

'Er, yes, I suppose so,' she told him absently, her glance riveted on the dark attractiveness of him that had taken her breath away and made her heart beat faster when they'd first met, and now had her crying inside all the time at the thought of shutting him out of her life.

If he was aware of the effect he was having on her, Hugo showed no sign of it. When Nathan had mentioned the dinner party he had guessed that the two doctors had arranged it to make the parting of the ways for Ruby and himself less painful and abrupt, and been grateful, even though he felt that their efforts would be futile.

The two of them would be taking the antenatal clinic later, as was usual on Mondays, and it would be the last time they did anything together, he thought as they separated without any further conversation.

As they dealt with the mothers-to-be in their different stages of pregnancy, some of them blooming and enjoying every moment of the amazing thing that was happening to them, and others with problems such as high blood pressure that had to be watched carefully, varicose veins, diabetes that had surfaced during the gestation period, to name a few, he saw how calm and reassuring Ruby was with the women who were nervous of the body changes they were experiencing.

And how while she was examining those who were sailing through the experience she listened patiently to their hopes and dreams for the future, when her own was so uncertain.

She was a gem and with the thought of the jewel she was named after he wondered what she'd done with the ring, and surmised that it would be stuffed at the back of a drawer somewhere out of sight.

It hurt him to think that when he'd asked her to marry him she hadn't given him the chance to choose between having her as a wife with no children from the marriage or taking the way out she was offering and ending the relationship. It had been a matter of her accepting that he would want a family first and foremost and with regard to that she'd proved to be unmovable.

When the clinic was over he said, 'You have just the right approach with our pregnant patients, don't miss a thing with regard to their general health and wellbeing, yet...' He paused and she knew what was coming next, 'You don't ever want to be in that position yourself?'

Not much! she thought grimly, but it was only to be expected that Hugo would see her recent behaviour in that light, and with a shrug of the shoulders she told him, 'Maybe it's because I always seemed to be on the maternity wards when we were sent out to do hospital-based training, and now I'm in the clinic here so...'

The nurse came in to clear away at that moment and with the second surgery of the day looming they separated and went to greet those in the waiting room with their various complaints.

The evenings of that last week in Swallowbrook passed as they had done for the last three, with Ruby down by the lake, drinking in every inch of its beauty to remember it by, and Hugo watching her set off with increasing impatience.

It was as if she was playing some sort of game with him, he thought. Was there no sorrow in her because she was leaving Swallowbrook and him, who it would seem was of less importance as she never came near *him* in the evenings.

On the Friday lunchtime she provided sandwiches and cakes and assorted savouries for the staff and everyone tucked in except Hugo who felt they would choke him. Afterwards he watched grim-faced, trying to ignore the tears on her lashes, as Libby presented her with a bouquet of flowers from them all, and then it was back to work on her last day at the Swallowbrook Medical Practice.

That evening he decided he'd had enough. He'd watched Ruby set off for the lake once again and began to follow her at a distance, determined to get at the truth of whether she loved him or not. If she admitted that she did he would want some answers regarding where her aversion to family life had come from.

He'd thought sometimes that it might have arisen from when her baby brother had been born with so many years between them. That maybe he'd been the centre of her parents' attention and she'd been pushed to one side, which had given her a jaundiced view of family life. Yet he could tell that Ruby loved her family from the way she spoke about them, so he couldn't see it being anything like that.

On the other hand, if she said that she *didn't* love him, at least he would know where he stood, as nothing could be worse than not knowing.

She was out of sight by the time he was ready to follow her and on his way Hugo had to pass the park, which was empty except for Sarah Bellingham seated on a bench, feeding the birds.

He made to hurry past but she'd seen him and called across 'Dr Lawrence, can you spare a moment?'

Groaning inwardly, he went across to her and concealing his impatience asked pleasantly, 'What can I do for you, Mrs Bellingham?'

'You remember that day when you and Dr Hollister came to my house? It was when the nurse was there and she'd been bossing me about...'

'Er, yes, I remember,' he told her hastily.

'And do you recall me asking Dr Hollister about her young brother who'd been poorly at the time they left Swallowbrook?'

'I remember something like that, but didn't take much notice as it all happened long before I came to live here, and if you'll excuse me I am in rather a hurry.'

He was turning, ready to leave, but she hadn't finished and was not going to let him go until she had.

Ignoring what he'd said, she went on to say, 'I remembered afterwards what was wrong with him. The child had that bleeding illness. He cut himself badly on some broken glass and it wouldn't stop bleeding. Like a slaughterhouse it was, but Dr John was onto it, knew what it was, had the ambulance there straight away, and the tests they took showed that he was right.'

'I see,' Hugo said slowly, a glimmer of light appearing in the midst of his confusion, and it was coming from a most unexpected source, but he had to put Sarah off the track to protect Ruby if there should be any truth in what she was saying, so he said casually, 'Yes, but I remember that Dr Hollister said that her brother is fine now, so maybe it was a false alarm of long ago as, like she said, everything seems to be all right now, so I would put it out of your mind.'

And contrite that he hadn't enquired about how her new hip was working he chatted for a few moments more then, desperate to be by himself as his mind grappled with what the old lady had told him in all innocence, he left her still feeding the birds and went back to Lakes Rise to think about what he was going to say to John Gallagher.

Incredible thoughts were crowding his mind, yet they were strangely believable, and before he saw Ruby again he needed some answers.

The lake had no appeal tonight, thought Ruby as she walked back to the apartment with dragging steps. She'd gone there each night to find solace and to stop herself from weakening in her resolve to stay away from Hugo until she was on her way home, but tonight she just wanted to be near him, to see him, and instead of going straight into the apartment she went across to the house.

She knew she would see him tomorrow at the dinner party, but they wouldn't be alone there. Libby and Nathan's invitation had been something she couldn't refuse. She'd known she ought to, that it would be a painful pleasure to take her leave of Hugo in such beautiful surroundings, but it was one more chance to be near him before she left the village on Sunday evening, and now that the time for her departure had come, every moment near him was not to be missed.

Lakes Rise was in darkness, no car on the drive, and disappointment was like a bitter taste in her mouth. Yet why should she expect him to be there just because she was suddenly desperate to be near him? She'd stayed well away from him every other evening and *he'd* kept out of *her* comings and goings, but now on a last desperate whim she wanted him and he wasn't there.

* * *

John was seated in his garden, watching the sun go down at the end of a beautiful day, and when Hugo pulled up outside the lodge on the riverbank he got to his feet and observed him in surprise.

The two men were on good terms. The elderly GP liked and respected Hugo, but he wasn't a regular visitor and neither did he usually look so grim.

'Want can I get you, Hugo?' he asked. 'Tea, coffee or a glass of wine maybe?'

Hugo shook his head. 'Nothing, John, thanks just the same. I'm here seeking information.'

'What about?' he asked, and pointed to a garden chair nearby. 'Make yourself comfortable.'

'I'm too tense to relax,' he said sombrely. 'You, John, are the first person to know that I've asked Ruby to marry me and received a very definite refusal, which I would have had to accept gracefully if she'd said it was because she wasn't in love with me. But the reason she gave was connected with the fact that she doesn't want children and knowing that I would want a family she felt that it wouldn't be fair to me if she married me.

'I felt at the time that if she loved me as much as I love her it would be for me to decide if I wanted to accept her views on family life. I still do feel like that, but she is adamant that she won't marry me and I need some answers.'

'And you've come to me?' his listener said heavily.

'Yes, because I think you might have the answer that I'm looking for. Ruby has been going down to the lake each evening to get away from me, I presume, and tonight, with only forty-eight hours before she leaves

Swallowbrook, I set off to follow her, determined to find out once and for all what is going on that I don't know about.

'On my way down there Sarah Bellingham accosted me. She was in the park, feeding the birds, and out of the blue told me that when Ruby's young brother was rushed into hospital all that time ago it was because he had what Sarah described as the bleeding illness, and light began to dawn.

'Is it right what she says, John? You were his doctor at that time, weren't you?'

He sighed. 'I'd rather you asked your questions of Ruby herself, Hugo. I can understand your desperation, but it is something that you have to clarify between the two of you, face to face, as it puts her in a very difficult position having to answer questions about something that she obviously hasn't wanted to discuss. I suggest you go and find her and treat her gently, whatever the outcome of your meeting.'

'You're right,' he said heavily. 'It was wrong of me to want to involve you in our affairs. I'll try down by the lake and if Ruby isn't there will wait for her back at Lakes Rise until she appears, no matter how long it takes.'

He was poised to leave and the other man said, 'It isn't that I wouldn't want to help you both find some happiness, Hugo, but I feel that it is a very private thing that you want some answers for, and that as I only knew a small part of it am better not interfering. So good luck to you both, and let us hope that Sarah Bellingham's chatter tonight might result in bringing some clarity to

Ruby's feelings for you. If it does, will you still want to marry her?'

'Yes, more than ever, knowing that the woman I love is willing to put my happiness before her own at such sacrifice, but she's got it wrong, John, without her I will never *be* happy.'

He was halfway down the path with his hand on the gate latch as he said, 'Thanks for your time. When we meet at the ferry tomorrow to sail across for the dinner party I hope to have Ruby's answer.'

'And that it's the one you want, eh?' was the reply. 'May the gods be good to you, Hugo.'

When he arrived back at the house it was his turn to find the person he was desperate to see not available. There were no lights on in the apartment and when he rang the bell there was no Ruby opening the door to him, so she had either gone to bed or hadn't come back from the lake, and as daylight had now turned to dusk if she didn't appear within seconds he would be off down there to seek her out.

He rang the bell again several times and as he was turning away the door opened and she was there with a robe over a short satin nightdress, obviously either having got out of bed to answer the urgent ringing down below or having been on her way upstairs.

Ruby had just reached the top when he'd rung the first time and had stood motionless on the landing, hoping he would go away. Her previous desperation to be with Hugo had gone. In his absence she'd had the chance to face up to the futility of any further contact between them, and now just wanted sleep to come and take her into the last hours of her life in Swallowbrook without any more hurt, but it was not to be, she thought as she stood back to let him into the darkened apartment.

The first thing Hugo did was switch on the lights. He wanted to see Ruby's expression when he asked her the question that was filling his mind.

Taking her hand, he led her into the lounge without either of them having yet spoken and when she was seated he stood looking down at her gravely, and in that moment she knew she couldn't leave the village without everything being straight and truthful between them, no matter what he said, or what he did afterwards, as nothing could be worse than denying Hugo what he was entitled to know.

'Hugo, I can't go without telling you the truth,' she told him. 'I've kept it from you long enough because I couldn't face the telling of it, but I need things to be honest and straightforward between us before I leave this place.' She took a deep breath and rising to stand before him said, 'The reason I don't want children and can't marry you is because…'

'You've got the haemophilia gene,' he said gently, and saw the colour drain from her face and her eyes grow huge in the whiteness of it.

'Who has told you that?' she whispered.

'No one. A chance remark made in all innocence set me thinking and the more I thought about it, the more it seemed believable, so is it true, Ruby? I have to know.'

'Yes, it's true,' she said wearily. '*That* is why I can't

marry you, Hugo. I can't deny you what should be rightfully yours because you feel sorry for me, or at this moment might think that my problem doesn't matter, because one day it will matter a lot.'

'And you were prepared to walk out of my life, throw away what we've got, without my opinion being asked?' he said gently. 'How could you do that to me, Ruby?'

'I once told a guy that I was dating about the faulty gene. He was a medical student like I was and he dropped me like a hot potato. When I met you I couldn't face the hurt of it happening again because I'd met the love of my life.'

'And so you feel that what you are doing is the least hurtful thing?'

'It has to be, hasn't it?'

Apart from holding her hand as he led her into the sitting room, he hadn't touched her so far, but it wasn't for the want of doing so. He ached to hold her close and bring Ruby the comfort and reassurance of *his* love for *her*, but first he had to say his piece, make sure that she wasn't going to feel anything other than cherished beyond her wildest dreams.

'You are beautiful and generous,' he told her, 'ready to give up on love for my sake and the children that you won't put at risk, but if we don't have any of our own, what is to stop us from caring for the children of others? There are children everywhere who desperately need loving parents, either through adoption or fostering. We have an example of the joy that can bring to both the child and those who have chosen to care for them in Toby, happy and contented with Libby and Nathan.'

'And you would be content to do something like that?' she asked in slow wonderment. 'You once said that you would like a house full of children like Toby, but were referring to children of your own flesh and blood.'

'Maybe I was, but we could still have happiness and fulfilment in the way I've suggested. I love you, Ruby, love everything about you, and want to be there for you every step of the way for the rest of our lives. So will you marry me? If you've given the ring to a charity or dispensed with it some other way, we can soon replace it.'

'Yes. I will marry you, Hugo,' she told him tremulously, 'and we don't have to replace the ring.' She slipped the robe off her shoulders, and he saw that beneath it, around her neck, was the chain, and on it centrally placed was the ring, as close to her heart as she could get it.

He held out his arms and she went into them on wings of joy and delighted disbelief as he took the chain gently from around her neck and slipped the ruby ring off it and onto her finger.

Her pallor had gone, her eyes were sparkling, she was glowing like the gemstone she was named after. He raised his eyes to heaven and gave thanks for the treasure in his arms that he had so nearly lost.

When they met John at the lakeside the following day, where Nathan was going to pick them up in his boat to take them to the island, the older man's glance went to the ring on Ruby's finger and said, 'So the gods *were* good, Hugo?'

'Yes, they were good,' he replied, with Ruby smiling up at him. 'More than I ever dreamed they could be.'

When Nathan came chugging alongside in his boat to take them to the island and heard their good news he was on the phone to Libby on the island straight away, asking her to have champagne ready.

Her response was, 'Wow! Fantastic! We've still got our clever young doctor, then?'

'It would seem so,' he told her, beaming across at them.

Ruby and Hugo made their wedding plans that night, strolling around the island in moonlight. Summer would be well advanced by the time they could make the necessary arrangements with the vicar and the caterers, but they didn't mind. They were going to be together for the rest of their lives and that was what mattered.

Nathan was to be Hugo's best man, Toby a page boy for the second time, and a friend of Ruby's from university was to be her bridesmaid.

On the home front Robbie would be an usher and her father would give her away. They'd rung her parents the night before to tell them their good news and her mother especially had rejoiced because the love of her daughter's life was a man who from the sound of it would never demand anything of her that she couldn't give, and who adored her as much as she did him. For the first time in years the burden of guilt that Jess carried around with her had lifted because the blight in their family was going to be wiped out in the present generation.

Her father had been just as happy to hear her news as her mother had been, but had said when they'd finished the call that he would feel better when he'd met the doctor that his daughter had given her heart to. She was very precious and had already had misery in her life. If Hugo could help take away the pain of what the fates had done to her, he also would rejoice.

The wedding banquet was to be held at Lakes Rise. Ruby and Hugo were hoping that the sun would shine on them, but even if it didn't, nothing could take the edge off their delight in each other.

It was hazy in the morning but by midday the golden ball was shining in the sky, and her mother and her bridesmaid smiled at Ruby in her wedding dress of cream satin and lace. Hugo, Nathan, Robbie and her father were making their way to the church resplendent in their male finery, and there was a satisfied smile on the face of the father of the bride.

He approved wholeheartedly of the man who was going to marry his daughter. He knew that Hugo would love and cherish her.

The organ sprang into life with the joyful strains of the wedding march. The bride had arrived. As Hugo rose to his feet Ruby walked slowly to meet him, holding her father's arm, and when she stepped forward to be beside her bridegroom, tall, slender and beautiful on her special day, all those who loved her were rejoicing, most of all the man at her side who had taken her in out of the cold on a dark winter night.

* * * * *

Medical mini-series
Sydney Harbour Hospital

Welcome to the world of Sydney Harbour Hospital

From saving lives to sizzling seduction,
these doctors are the very best!

Sydney Harbour Hospital: Lily's Scandal
by Marion Lennox
Sydney Harbour Hospital: Zoe's Baby
by Alison Roberts
On sale 3rd February

Sydney Harbour Hospital: Luca and the Bad Girl
by Amy Andrews
On sale 2nd March

Sydney Harbour Hospital: The Pride of Dr Tom Jordan
by Fiona Lowe
On sale 6th April

Sydney Harbour Hospital: The Socialite's Secret
by Melanie Milburne
On sale 4th May

Sydney Harbour Hospital: Shrinking Violet's Guide to Life
by Emily Forbes
On sale 1st June

Sydney Harbour Hospital: The Untamed Italian
by Fiona McArthur
On sale 6th July

Sydney Harbour Hospital: Fixing Ava's Marriage
by Carol Marinelli
On sale 3rd August

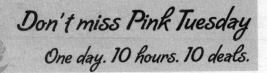